Street of the Seven Angels

Works by John Howard Griffin

The Devil Rides Outside (1952)

Nuni (1956)

Land of the High Sky (1959)

Black Like Me (1961)

The John Howard Griffin Reader (1968)

The Church and the Black Man (1969)

*A Hidden Wholeness:
The Visual World of Thomas Merton* (1970)

Twelve Photographic Portraits (1973)

*Jacques Maritain:
Homage in Words and Pictures* (1974)

A Time to Be Human (1977)

The Hermitage Journals (1981)

*Follow the Ecstasy:
Thomas Merton's Hermitage Years* (1983, 1993)

Pilgrimage (1985)

Encounters with the Other (1997)

Street of the Seven Angels (2003)

Street of the Seven Angels

John Howard Griffin

Edited and with an Introduction by

Robert Bonazzi

San Antonio, Texas
2003

Street of the Seven Angels © 2003
by Susan Griffin-Campbell, John H. Griffin, Jr.
Gregory Parker Griffin and Amanda Griffin-Fenton

Introduction © 2003 by Robert Bonazzi

First Edition

ISBN: 0-930324-74-9 (hardcover edition)

Wings Press
627 E. Guenther
San Antonio, Texas 78210
Phone/fax: (210) 271-7805

On-line catalogue and ordering:
www.wingspress.com

Library of Congress Cataloging-in-Publication data:

Griffin, John Howard, 1920 - 1980
        Street of the Seven Angels / John Howard Griffin
                p.   cm.
        ISBN: 0-930324-74-9 (hc)
(non acidic paper)
        1. Censorship – France – fiction. 2. Paris
(France) – Fiction. I. Bonazzi, Robert.
PS3557.R489S87   2003
813.54

Dedicated to

Gregory and Amanda

Introduction

Robert Bonazzi

John Howard Griffin's third novel, *Street of the Seven Angels*, was not published during his lifetime [1920-1980]. After *Black Like Me* had become a best-selling paperback during the sixties, his life changed dramatically from being a solitary novelist to that of a celebrated public lecturer and essayist on race-relations. Griffin wrote only one work of fiction after 1961—the short story *Pilgrimage*—published posthumously by his widow, the late Elizabeth Griffin-Bonazzi, as a chapbook with Latitudes Press in 1985.

Like his two published novels—*The Devil Rides Outside* (Smiths, 1952) and *Nuni* (Houghton Mifflin, 1956)—*Street of the Seven Angels* was composed during Griffin's decade of sightlessness, 1947 to 1957. All three novels draw upon classical music for their forms: *The Devil Rides Outside* is based on Beethoven's Opus 131 String Quartet; *Nuni* is a dissonant, contrapuntal work with a single voice line; and *Street of the Seven Angels* takes its shape from the sonatas of Mozart.

Drafted in 1955—and revised in 1961 after he had recovered eyesight—*Street* is a finely-crafted novel wherein "every scene has its answering scene," Griffin explained. By alternating jubilant scenes with somber ones, it maintains a Mozartean balance of phrase and response. "In fact," he added, "I played Mozart continually during the writing and rewriting of this novel, and anywhere the tone of the work did not coincide with the tone of the music, I changed the work."

Classical music was his first and life-long artistic fascination. As a musicologist and lecturer on music history, Griffin realized that he had "studied music so much that it destroyed creativity in that area." He had dreamed of becoming a composer, but then "ended up learning every damned rule in the book," he lamented. "I knew everything you *could not do*, and this silenced me as a composer. I could write a technically correct work, but I was too constricted by the rules to breathe any life into it."

When he began writing fiction in 1947, Griffin decided "to avoid falling into that same trap. I still have a great love of form and technique," he admitted, "but the raw material comes initially from the flow that is largely an ability—usually under the stimulus of music—to allow the unconscious to speak. I did not set about learning to write at all. Rather, I took musical forms and constructed my fiction on them."

Unlike the two earlier novels—which are intensely realistic and deeply philosophical first-person narratives written in the present tense—*Street of the Seven Angels* is a satirical comedy written in the past tense from the omnipotent point of view. However, it does contain substantial levels of consideration, including a serio-comic discourse on censorship and pornography and an in-depth dialogue between common morality and uncommon spirituality.

The novel's theme, according to Griffin, "deals with the self-defeating hypothesis which do-gooder groups have—the compulsory return of the Kingdom of God on earth—and it deals with freedom of the will, in that any moral virtue which is compulsory therefore loses all value."

In *Street of the Seven Angels*, six pietistic women form The Society for the Preservation of Christian Morality Against Contemporary Indecency. They carry on their work, despite the efforts of their spiritual guide, the parish priest Father Trissotin, who scribbles religious tracts and advises them to tone it down a bit. They "behave with absolute missionary zeal," Griffin explained, "and through their actions demonstrate the absurdity of the censoring 'watchdog' mentality, particularly when it is exercised with such moral obtuseness."

Counterpointing the funny, catty scenes at the spinster Mailleferre's Religious Arts Shop, where the censorship group congregates to plot strategy, are those scenes in the Dominican novitiate that reveal the simple monastic life of prayer and silence. "You have a contrast between the asceticism, the love of truth in the spirit of Aquinas that goes on in this completely enclosed Dominican house," Griffin said, "and then you have this group muddling through all the obscenity and pornography they can find—to show the devastating effect they have for bad on this whole community, though they're under the horrible illusion they're cleaning it up."

This implied contrast between the enraged, opinionated censors and the enlightened, silent monks illuminates a related although unstated theme—"that moral virtue is impossible without the virtues of prudence and intelligence which lead us to the right way of achieving a good end." These Thomistic views, essential in all he wrote after his 1951 conversion to Catholicism—including *The Devil Rides Outside*, wherein the agnostic narrator argues against all religions—were among the theological, ethical and spiritual ideas that radicalized him during a decade of sightlessness.

"My concept of the faith is that no truth I can discover can possibly be in ultimate disharmony with the truth of the faith," Griffin said, paraphrasing Aquinas' bold proposition. However, even as he reshaped his texts to harmonize with musical forms, never did he realign the content with religious dogma.

"I have a very profound belief that the virtue of art is ultimately the greatest of all virtues. If I had to pervert my characters or what they say in order to make them harmonize with some tenet of the faith, I would never do it," he insisted. "If a character is doing or saying something I'm positive he would say or do—even though it's enormously offensive to me—I still do it. A work of art that's as true as you can make it, with your focus entirely on *the work* and on nothing else—not on side issues or your faith, not on your audience or on your self—then I believe this will ultimately produce health. This is the daring part of art to me."

Even though literary influences are not easily discernable in Griffin's earlier fiction, he indicated that his comedy had been influenced by the comedies of Molière, especially the scenes that allude to *Le Misanthrope*. Curiously, *Street* also suggests a cinematic sensibility in the arrangement of its 34 scenes that continue without pause. However, Griffin was not a movie-goer. In fact, he rarely read contemporary novels, since he was wary of being unconsciously imitative of modern fiction. His literary heroes were the classic French authors— Rabelais, Molière, Montaigne, Balzac, Flaubert, Stendhal— whose books he had studied as a teenager in search of a "classical education" at the Lycée Descartes in Tours, France.

The most obvious religious influence upon the novel's subtext will be found in the passages in Scene 26, wherein portions of Marcel de Corte's profound essay "Incarnation and Pseudo-Incarnation" are methodically intoned by the Dominican Reader in the sacristy of the empty church. Mademoiselle Mailleferre, leader of the *Société*, overhears the Reader's voice and, while initially rejecting this discourse on the false dualism of mind and soul, she begins to reconsider it.

Then she listens to Father Gregoire, the humble Dominican prior, who clarifies the meaning of the reading to his novices. He tells them that the true goal of the saints was in loving God and not in judging humanity; and that the key to sanctity was never to think evil of another, but to forgive the moralizers even though they tend to think evil of everyone except themselves. Listening to the inherent wisdom of Father Gregoire's clarifications stirs Mademoiselle Mailleferre to a religious epiphany.

This scene illuminates the core spiritual message and also exposes the logical fallacy of censorship. Griffin firmly believed this wisdom, which was explained to him by his first spiritual guide, Father Marie-Bruno, who was the inspiration for Father Gregoire in *Street of the Seven Angels*, as well as the model for the heroic Trappist monk, Brother Marie-Orno, in *The Devil Rides Outside*. Griffin was familiar with the novel's setting—the Saint Jacques district of Paris—for he had made a retreat to the Dominican novitiate, located at the

corner of Boulevard Saint Jacques and Street of the Seven
Angels, to visit with Father Marie-Bruno in 1946. This ancient
novitiate holds a unique place in Catholic history, because
such saints as Albert the Great, Aquinas and Bonaventura lectured there during the eleventh century.

In the 1955 draft of *Street* the time-frame was to be two
consecutive Tuesdays in the late forties or early fifties, but
when Griffin revised it in 1961, the comic-hero Charles
Durand establishes the time of action by linking it with the
1960 death of Pierre Reverdy and the edition of the poet's last
book of poetry, *La Liberté des mers*, illustrated by the cubist
painter Georges Braque. Along with these legendary French
modernists, Thomist philosopher Jacques Maritain and
Dominican theologian Father Gerald Vann are among several
Griffin friends mentioned in the novel.

There are other autobiographical references. The
novel's courtroom arguments were based on transcripts from
the Detroit censorship trial of the paperback version of *The
Devil Rides Outside* (Pocket Books, 1954). He also modeled
his do-gooder's *Société* on The Legion for Decent Literature,
the Catholic organization which had been the most aggressive
force in banning his novel. The Detroit decision was over-
turned in 1956 by the U.S. Supreme Court, which judged the
novel not to be obscene in the landmark decision (*Butler v.
Michigan*). Speaking for the majority, Justice Felix
Frankfurter's opinion established that no book was to be
banned merely on the basis of selected words or passages
taken out of context, and that all books had to be evaluated in
their entirety.

"Art, in order to have any influence on understanding, must
exist whole," Griffin wrote. "This statute denied the existence
of that essential quality of wholeness, and allowed a book to be
declared obscene because of words taken out of context, which
was like judging one's soul by a hand severed from his body in
an anatomy lab."

The decision also clarified that books could not be

banned because such adult content might fall into the hands of children. "Must serious novelists, who wish to treat essentially adult emotions and problems," Griffin asked rhetorically, "aim their dramatic incidents through the filter of juvenile concepts and capacities? Can there be no such thing as an essentially adult fiction? The ramifications of such a statute are staggering, for logically everything from the *Bible* through the world's great classics would or could be banned on this basis. How I despise this puritanical-Jansenist trend that turns spiritual health into a type of acidly hygienic destruction," he concluded, "which seeks only to kill in the hope that virtue will somehow be left intact in the vacuum; seeing as evil those things which God saw as good."

While these points are made indirectly in *Street*—its comic hero, the bookseller Durand, is the defendant—the banning of literature is not the trial's central focus. Instead *Street* makes light fun of so-called pornography, even while Griffin's serious essays and public statements on censorship passionately defended intellectual and artistic freedom.

Durand has been accused of defacing a statue of *The Reclining Diana*, a public monument covered with graffiti for decades. He claims to have been erasing not making obscene marks when apprehended. But "Durand thinks she is a big howl," Griffin noted, "and he can never decide if she is lying there on her marble pedestal spread-eagled waiting for her lover or her gynecologist."

Street also makes light of musical references, including one extended joke that echoes the names the French composers once known as *Les Six* of Paris during the twenties. By simply changing the first letter of each composer's last name, each reformer's last name becomes a musical joke. Thus, the widows Ponneger and Duric derive from Arthur Honneger and Georges Auric; Mesdames Hilhaud and Aurey from Darius Milhaud and Louis Durey; and the spinsters Mailleferre and Toulenc from Germain Tailleferre and Francis Poulenc. What Griffin had intended as a specific send-up of his Parisian acquaintances Milhaud and Poulenc, perhaps necessitates a footnote today—80 years after the six younger composers made their only joint recording to honor their elder French composer Erik Satie.

Griffin's legacy would have met the same footnoted fate if not for the usefulness of *Black Like Me* as a teaching text about white racism during the segregation era and the popularity of *Follow the Ecstasy* (Orbis, 1993), his memoir about the last years of Trappist monk and author Thomas Merton. These nonfiction works are the only two of Griffin's 15 titles in print. The earlier novels have been unavailable since their inclusion, as condensed by editor Bradford Daniel, in *The John Howard Griffin Reader* (Houghton Mifflin, 1968). The classic *Black Like Me* has been translated into 14 languages since its original appearance in 1961. It has sold over 11 million copies, has never been out of print in English or French, remains available in a 35th anniversary paperback edition (Signet, 1996), and is being reissued in 2003 by New American Library in a trade paperback edition with a new cover.

Street of the Seven Angels was originally under contract to Houghton Mifflin, but the Boston firm decided not to publish it since *Nuni* had poor sales and was not reprinted by a paperback house—despite excellent reviews and the international success of his first novel. *The Devil Rides Outside* had been a bestseller in France and England, and later became a paperback bestseller in the States. The publisher, along with other firms in New York and Toronto which read the manuscript after Griffin's death, were of the opinion that *Street* was "too sophisticated" or "too French" for North American readers, since the story was set in Paris, replete with references thoroughly Parisian but without any American characters.

Yet, *The Devil Rides Outside*, set in a Benedictine monastery nestled in a provincial French village, contains but one American, the musicologist who narrates the 600-page novel. For that matter, the only American in *Nuni* is John Harper, the stranded professor who narrates the 300-page allegorical tale about an aboriginal tribe on a remote Pacific island.

In a letter to the literary historian Maxwell Geismar, who brought national attention to Griffin's novels in *American Moderns* in 1958, Griffin discussed *Street* and its themes. "It deals with the mentality of censorship—the book-banners, the guardians of public virtue, or 'the sanctimonious serpents,' as Gerald Vann called them." He continued by saying that, "underlying this, counterpointing it, though the themes never touch, is a subsidiary plot and a list of characters, an essentially somber one. *Street* is almost entirely written in scenes with very little introspection. It lays the foundation for *Passacaglia* [another of his unpublished novels], which comes right out with the idea that morality is an unamiable goal in itself, that it will calcify the soul of anyone who aims at the perfection of routine Christian morality."

Griffin had initially envisioned *Street* and *Passacaglia* as one massive work, but after multiple drafts he created two separate novels. They share the Paris setting, one main character (Father Gregoire), and a few minor ones. And once again, the form was drawn from classical music and the thematics echoed Thomist theology.

This fourth novel—predicated on the passacaglia, a dance form introduced into keyboard music early in the 17th century—explores the art and life of Paul Gallois, a concert pianist. Like Durand, the bookseller in *Street*, Gallois is not a religious man. As Griffin wrote to Geismar, he "would be considered unmoral by the dogmatic standards of morality—the sort of dead morality that tends to destroy the naturally functioning human being and is, in fact, an obscenity."

Griffin concluded that "in order to move beyond this routine morality, one must undo the damage, the concretization of soul which can neither grow nor dilate into those areas that in theology we call sanctity, in psychology integration, and in art genius."

Passacaglia equates the spirituality of the artist with the spirituality of the authentically religious. In this case, the dedicated pianist (Gallois) attains parallel spirituality with the humble priest (Father Gregoire)—created from the novelist's experience of music mentors who imbued him with the meaning of artistic dedication and religious guides who revealed in their behavior a genuine humility.

For this novelist-musicologist, the true artist "lives constantly in the highest realms of art, with the greatest utterances of Bach, Mozart and Beethoven, which has a parallel effect to what even the greatest mystical life has." Griffin made this point often in interviews and letters, and it is dramatized in his fiction, specifically the connection made between Gregorian Chant and the mysticism in the monastic scenes of both *The Devil Rides Outside* and *Street of the Seven Angels*.

Each novel features scenes from a medieval cloister, symbolic of the eternal, juxtaposed with scenes from the outside world. In *The Devil*, the cloister contrasts with the village and in *Street*, it contrasts the city. Both the village and the city represent the fallen state of temporal society. In the first novel, "the devil rides outside monastery walls," according to the French proverb; in *Street*, evil resides not in the marble statue of a nude goddess or in erotic literature, but in the obscenity of censorship.

Griffin was no stranger to the history of modern censorship and, due to the landmark legal case involving his own controversial novel, he had been a part of that history. His involvement in subsequent debates during the 1960s, including several challenges to *Black Like Me* that were dismissed by lower courts, did not place him in the vortex as the controversial test case had. Nonetheless, his role as critic was no less passionate; and he controlled his outrage, if not his outrageous humor, by approaching the subject with objective research, logical analysis, ethical scrutiny and historical perspective.

There are moments of humor in *The Devil Rides Outside* and *Nuni* but the tone of their social satire is serious. The satire in *Street* is equally on target, but bawdy and delightful.

To those who knew Griffin, the portly Charles Durand appears to be a self-deprecating parody of his creator, who also stood up for artistic expression, baked delicious bread for local monks, and argued with his mother-in-law about the nature of free will.

Most of today's readers will not know of Griffin's previously published novels, and just a few editors have read *Street* in manuscript form. Only one portion was anthologized—as a short story under the title "Chez Durand"—in the New World Writing series published by New American Library in 1957. And, except for Geismar's *American Moderns* and studies by Decherd Turner, Eugene McNamara and Jeff Campbell, his novels had received superficial reviews in the national press.

Perhaps the most remembered reaction—for Texans especially—was registered by the popular Texas novelist Larry McMurtry in his piece, "Ever A Bridegroom: Reflections on the Failure of Texas Literature," published in *The Texas Observer* in 1981, the year after Griffin's death.

McMurtry included *The Devil Rides Outside*—with *Goodbye to a River* by John Graves, *The Ordways* by William Humphrey and *The House of Breath* by William Goyen—as being "among our very best books." About *The Devil Rides Outside*, he said: "It is a strange, strong book whose verbal energy—a quality very rare in our fiction—still seems remarkable after almost 30 years. In the mostly all-too-healthy and sunlit world of Texas fiction, the book remains an anomaly, dark, feverish, introverted, claustrophobic, tortured."

McMurtry also quipped that *"The Devil Rides Outside* has the lonely distinction of being the best French novel ever published in Fort Worth." This was a reference to the fact that the novel set in France had been published in Fort Worth by Smiths, Inc. These were not the "coughdrop kings," as Geismar had joked, but Fort Worth businessmen, the brothers J. Hulbert and Gordon Smith (who edited the novel with Griffin in 1949).

Then McMurtry went on to dismiss Griffin and his work

in a series of unenlightened opinions: "It [*The Devil Rides Outside*] was so complete and so explosive an outpouring of intellectualized emotion that Griffin seemed, from then on, a sort of emptied man. His second novel, *Nuni*, had neither energy nor force. He then wrote a history of a Midland bank, and finally, perhaps in desperation, turned himself black, in a last effort to find something strong to write about."

What might "intellectualized emotion" be—projecting emotion with one's head but not feeling it in one's heart? How could McMurtry know that Griffin was "a sort of emptied man" merely from cataloging the late author's books which he seemed not to have read carefully, or at all? *Nuni* has an undeniable energy and force that cannot be missed, even if one was not drawn to its dark allegory or one had misunderstood the meaning of its spiritual subtext. And Griffin never wrote "a history of a Midland bank," but instead an engaging history of the *llano estacado*—the staked plains region of West Texas, *Land of the High Sky* (1959), which was produced by a Midland bank in a limited clothbound edition.

But certainly, no indication emerges—after researching his life and work over three decades—to suggest that he had embarked "in desperation" upon the *Black Like Me* journey "in a last effort to find something strong to write about."

First, Griffin had decided to risk the experiment because he felt under obedience to the sacredness of human life as a devout Roman Catholic; and he was moved by the ethical challenge of his spiritual mentor, Jacques Maritain, who had called on fellow Catholics to make personal sacrifices in the human rights struggle for all. Second, what eventually evolved into *Black Like Me* had been intended as a sociological study to determine the extent and effect of white racism upon black people in the segregated Deep South in 1959. But never was it an attempt, desperate or otherwise, to discover new experiences about which to write. His works-in-progress—including *Scattered Shadows*, a memoir about his years of sightlessness and sight-recovery, plus the novels *Passacaglia* and *Street*—

do not lack power or significance. (For an account of this period, see *Man in the Mirror: John Howard Griffin and the Story
of Black Like Me*, published by Orbis Books in 1997, and still
in print.)

A starkly contrasting view and tone are evident in Decherd
Turner's essay about *The John Howard Griffin Reader*. "My
claims for the work of John Howard Griffin are not extrava-
gant. They're just universal," wrote Turner in his 1968 *Dallas
Times-Herald* review. "He has the poetic gifts and graces to
capture the eternal struggle of a man to know his own soul. He
has . . . the skill of a master-confessor who, with exquisite
casuistry, elicits the intertwined skeins of slave and saint in
everyman. No living artist has drawn such classic and extensive contours around his work." This was the response of a
metropolitan book editor and rare book expert to Griffin's
588-page compendium that could hardly be characterized
accurately as the output of "a sort of emptied man." However,
McMurtry's assertion that he had "an odd, lop-sided career"
as a novelist was true, but not because Griffin had "been
pressed into fiction by the force of one compelling traumatic
experience," or that he had "the always serious, usually fatal
misfortune to write his best book first." Rather, his "misfortune" had been due to the unexpected success of *Black Like
Me*, which provided a platform to speak out against racism
and human rights abuses during the sixties and seventies. That
career, begun in his forties, made it possible to support his
large family and to pay the astronomical medical expenses of a
life-long battle against the ravaging complications of diabetes.

On the other hand, the extensive travel had kept him
away from his studio and the solitude necessary to compose
novels of significance. He had not written merely to entertain,
but always endeavored to illuminate a spiritual vision in fiction. Yet, he was not against being entertaining in the process,
as the multi-leveled *Street* demonstrates with its old world
charm, modern wit and biting social satire.

"My fiction is permeated with the profoundest belief,"

Griffin wrote to novelist Lillian Smith in a 1961 letter, "that art and man's gift of himself to his daemon, no matter what his superficial personal life and beliefs, restores to him the inno-cence of mystery; and restores it also to the world, in that it allows, in Heraclitus' phrase, humanity to look into the essences of things and to encounter the mystery. It seeks, by implication only, to show how art and the artist re-establish in the subtlest way a hierarchy of values that the world is always losing, [how they] restore the clarity of the *ordo universali* from which we are always skittering toward our suicide; and within this, reveals the basic obscenity of our standards of modesty and delusion."

By *ordo universali* Griffin meant, of course, the univer-sal order that remains a mystery when we contemplate its essence rather than presume to know it only by appearance. He was appalled by the politico-economic notions of the New World Order—a global creed of greed that remains insensitive to human rights and also "reveals the basic obscenity of our standards," controlled by wealth and power but without ethics or values.

Will this sophisticated satire, which never dictates but simply personifies its meaning through the actions of its varied characters, be too serious for the sitcom and dot.com genera-tions? Perhaps not, since now one need not be a Francophile to be appreciative of things either French or liberating.

Will *Street* have "the lonely distinction of being the best French novel ever published" in San Antonio? No, because Wings Press has attracted an international list of authors like few other independents, discovering and re-discovering quali-ty literary works that the decaying establishment ceased understanding or caring about decades ago.

Street of the Seven Angels transports John Howard Griffin's literary vision into the new millennium, embodying a satiric wit which exposes the ugly while exalting the humane. It brings to the library of the living a neglected work by a dynamic, original, and deeply spiritual 20th century writer, who transcended the hatred of his attackers with the wisdom of fraternal love and genuine humility.

And now he laughs with the angels.

Acknowledgments

An earlier version of Scene 17 appeared in *New World Writing 12* (NY: New American Library, 1957); excerpts from Marcel de Corte's essay in Scene 26, translated by Cicily Hastings, were reprinted from *Conflict and Light* (London/New York: Sheed and Ward. The cover art, "Moses" (oil on canvas, 1955), was published in *Abraham Rattner, (Urbana:* University of Illinois Press, 1956). Thanks are extended to these publishers for permission to reprint.

Wings Press thanks librarians Lucy E. Duncan of St. Phillip's College and John Conyers of the University of Texas at San Antonio for help with cataloging.

PART ONE

THE FIRST TUESDAY

However innocent a thing may be,
men can still discover a crime in it.

— Molière

1

"It's almost five." Claudine called from the rear of Mademoiselle Mailleferre's Religious Arts Shop. "May I go now, Mademoiselle?"

"Did you hang the new scapulars on the rack?" Mademoiselle Mailleferre asked.

"Yes, Mademoiselle . . ."

The proprietress bent her tall figure slightly forward and peered through the cluttered gloom toward her helper.

"Did you arrange Father Trissotin's pamphlets on the display stand?"

Claudine's work-rough hand flew to her mouth.

"Where's your mind, child?" Mademoiselle sighed. She rubbed her fingertips into her temples. "Well, run fix them, and then you can go."

Dear God, there were still a thousand things to do before tonight's meeting.

"Arrange them neatly," she called to Claudine. "Put them on top of the other booklets. Father Trissotin will be here tonight and I don't want him to think I'm not pushing his . . ."

"I am, Mademoiselle," the girl sang out.

The proprietress turned toward the front display window and glanced out into the narrow rain-slicked street. Behind her she heard the rapid shuffle of pamphlets and snatches of that popular song Claudine frequently hummed.

Now what? She would have to build a little fire in the furnace so the ladies would have some heat when they met in her upstairs salon. And tea for them. And she'd have to go out in the vile weather and buy butter cookies and tarts. Impossible to trust Claudine with such a mission. She started past the shoulder of a life-size plaster statue of St. Joseph. Through her rain-stippled window she watched men in berets carry long loaves of unwrapped bread under their arms as they hurried to get their aperitifs before going home to supper. The Cafe Zeus around the corner on Boulevard St. Jacques would be rushed for the next hour. By the same token, the green metal public urinal down on the corner, in the center promenade of the boulevard, would have a constant stream of men.

A gray draft horse, its back slick with rain, strained to pull a coal cart up the steep incline past her shop. The rattle of metal-rimmed wheels on cobblestones overwhelmed the tinkle of her entry bell when the door beside her opened.

Her eyes dulled. She nodded briefly to old Flamart, the stone mason.

"The little one is still here?" he asked, shoving his beret back respectfully.

"In the back."

"Grandpapa!" Claudine cried with an enthusiasm that Mademoiselle found almost unendurable. The girl ran forward between counters of rosaries, missals and ceramic statues of the Sacred Heart. She hugged the old man and then stood back to admire him.

"How handsome you are!"

Mademoiselle heard Flamart laugh with embarrassment.

"You've been to the baths?"

"No," he snorted as though the question were somehow insulting.

"But you smell so . . ."

"I just went over to the Breville Museum. I washed and changed clothes there."

"How?"

"In the men's room. It's nice there."

"You didn't!"

Mademoiselle turned back to the window and tried to ignore their gigglings and mutterings.

Honestly, she thought, wasn't that something to get excited about? An old man washes and changes clothes. It was said around the neighborhood that, despite his great age, he frequented Madame Culuhac's girls once a week. Mademoiselle had little doubt this was the night. She shut out the hint of tenderness for him and forced herself to be revolted. Anyway, was it not slightly unethical to bathe in the men's room of a public art museum? She craned to look up the street where the gray façade of the Breville Museum flaunted its Roman columns. She had only been inside once, seventeen years ago. And then she had not got past the foyer where a gigantic statue of Michelangelo's David rose naked in all its marble warmth beside the equally life-size figure of a Greek obscenity called The Reclining Diana. Her confessor, in view of her violently disturbed reaction—she had actually vomited—had suggested that she avoid the place for a while. Occasionally, in unguarded moments, the entire scene would appear before her eyes, as vivid now as it had been seventeen years ago when she first viewed it as a girl of twenty. She would recall with wonder the extraordinary manner in which the artist had made the veins in the marble match nature's veins in David's buttocks. She shook her head to rid herself of the uncomfortable vision.

"Take my work clothes home when you go this evening, eh petite?" she heard Flamart say.

"All right, Grandpapa—you sure smell good."

Mademoiselle Mailleferre closed out another image, this time of the old man standing in front of one of the basins in the Museum's men's room, grandly soaping himself with tax-purchased castile. Certainly it was meant for hand washing, not for cleansing the whole body. And what if some dignitary—a person like de Gaulle, or a Cardinal, or a venerable conductor—were to walk into the men's room and be confronted by such a sight? Would he reach past Flamart's wet nakedness and say "Pardon me, may I use the soap?" Not likely. It might not bother Flamart, but it would certainly give the dignitary a poor impression of the district.

Three small boys in heavy jackets and short pants attracted her attention back to the narrow street directly in front of her shop. They chalked MERDE on the soaked brick wall of the Dominican Novitiate. And you could be sure, Mademoiselle told herself, they would be right there at the altar rail next Sunday to take Christ Jesus into their little bodies.

With the exception of her shop and, to a lesser extent, those Dominicans across the street, the quarter was inhabited by this type. Most of them were earthbound humans of the most vulgar stamp, natural beings who worked all day and then purchased their bread and went home to their animal existence every evening. Had she not only last week noticed an article in the Figaro Litteraire which said it was not unusual for French couples to make love three times a day?

Not much depth in any of them.

Flamart loomed beside her, his hand on the door knob. He lifted the forefinger of his free hand to his white eyebrow in respectful salute. The typically peasant gesture touched Mademoiselle and she acknowledged it with a show of warmth in her smile.

The fresh rain-fragrance of ozone, mingled with castile surrounded Mademoiselle for a moment as Flamart opened the door, stepped out and closed it. She watched him hunch his shoulders against the drizzle and start away.

"Flamart!" someone called. The stone mason turned and peered up the narrow sidewalk. Almost immediately Mademoiselle saw Durand, the book shop owner, as fat and pink-cheeked as ever, stride into view beneath his black umbrella.

"You going to the cafe?" she heard Flamart ask as the two shook hands there only a few inches in front of her window.

"Yes, but I've got to piss first," Durand announced affably.

Mademoiselle, though invisible behind the rain-pocked glass, instinctively moved further behind the statue of St.

Joseph. Honestly, that Durand. He didn't care how he talked. You'd think, Mademoiselle told herself, that dealing in books would exert a refining influence on a man. But not Durand. Gossip had it he was gross in his dealings with women.

Absently she watched the two men angle across the street to the public urinal.

Let's see, there would be six women at the meeting, counting herself, plus Father Trissotin. (The leaves were almost gone from the trees on the boulevard, she observed sadly, as she watched Durand hand Flamart his umbrella, glance up at the dripping trees and start unbuttoning even before he stepped into the urinal.) A couple of dozen cookies and tarts would be enough. But still that lard-tub of a Madame Ponneger was one more glutton—a sure sign of fanaticism, she observed. But no, it wasn't her responsibility to fill that cavern. Two dozen cookies would have to do.

"May I go now, Mademoiselle? I've finished," Claudine called from the shadows.

"Yes, but first run downstairs and put one bucket of coal in the furnace. Then turn on the radiator upstairs in my salon."

Across the street, the milkman's two-wheeled cart, pulled by a wolf-like dog, stopped in front of the Dominican house.

Her gaze shifted back to the hazed figure of Flamart who waited patiently for his friend. She saw something pathetic, almost desolate in the scene. Yes, one couldn't help feeling some passion for Flamart, despite the weakness of his flesh.

Now Durand joined him. The bookseller waddled in a awkward semi-crouch as he worked with both hands to button his fly. Why they did not button up before appearing back in public was something Mademoiselle could not understand. Always it was the same. The only men who left such places with any semblance of dignity were clergymen and foreigners. This was so pronounced that whenever Mademoiselle saw a man leave without assuming that baboon stance she wondered what country he was from.

She thought of the Lenten Masses the Dominicans would soon be chanting, and a phrase came to her: "*Adhaesit in terra venter noster*—our bellies are as glued to the earth." It had always seemed to her such a coarse and unliturgical sort of phrase, but she saw it now as a remarkably apt description of the whole tenor of the quarter.

"Just one bucket, Claudine," she called down into the cellar.

"It won't give much heat, Mademoiselle."

"Just one. God's love, I'm not running a Turkish bath."

"Yes, Mademoiselle."

2

Montausier adjusted his fleshless over-long legs to some semblance of comfort beneath his chair. He glared at his mortal enemy and best friend, if one could call such a compromised character as Durand a friend, Lord.

"You're as disgusting as the rest," he snapped. "And I don't mind . . ."

"Please . . . please . . ." Durand said pleasantly.

The waiter placed two glasses of beer and one of red wine on the round metal table and then stepped back into the gloom to become part of the elbows and newspapers and chess games and chatter of the Cafe Zeus.

"Let's stop, just for once, denouncing the morals of this age," Durand resumed amiably. He relaxed his bulk back into the wire chair, nudged his gold-rimmed glasses up to the bridge of his nose and lifted his glass.

Someone opened the door, and the sudden racket of rain pouring against cobblestones made Montausier wait. Beyond the immediate splashing, they heard the deep-toned bell from the tower of the *Palais de Justice*. It sent its reverberating metallic tones slowly over the quarter, tolling five o'clock.

Montausier caught Flamart's eye, and nodded toward Durand. There he sat, guzzling his beer, his eyes smiling over the rim of his demi-glass in that speculative and affectionate way of his toward a nice-looking girl across the room.

The bell's final echo was muffled by the closing door. Durand turned his attention back to Montausier's dark face, noticed that his elderly companion's moustache was not twitching yet, and resumed his goading.

"Really—such a rage against the morality of this age makes a man look slightly ridiculous. Don't you agree, old Flamart?"

Flamart's face congested with a blush and he shrugged his shoulders, embarrassed the way very simple men are with ideas—a silliness he had not concerned himself with in over forty years.

"Makes me look ridiculous, eh?" Montausier said. "By whose standards? By mankind's standards?" He stretched his head forward on his skinny neck and spread out his hands expansively. "But that's all I ask. Mankind is so stupid I should consider myself gravely at fault to be seen as wise in its eyes."

"Such a hatred for mankind," Durand sighed. He signaled the waiter again.

"Hatred no," Montausier specified. "Contempt yes. I have a general contempt for all mankind."

Flamart's blue eyes rolled to one side as if to say that this, just the same, was a bit exaggerated.

"All mankind?" Durand asked.

"All mankind," Montausier nodded. "The ones because they have no principles. And the others, like you, because you are complacent with them. To think that we could arrive at an age where one retains amicable relations with, even shows respect for, vice."

"Messieurs?" the waiter interrupted.

"What? Oh, another beer, please," Montausier said. "I

tell you," he went on leaning across the table toward Flamart and Durand, "there are times when I want to flee into the desert at the sight of my fellow man."

"Another beer, please," Durand said. He smiled at the waiter and then at Montausier, as though to explain that they must be indulgent with the old fool.

Montausier's knuckles blanched with the tight clasp of his hands. Durand was daring to apologize for him, one of the most distinguished lawyers of the district before his retirement. It was too admirable really. Too admirable.

Few men would go that far without quailing.

Flamart indicated a repeat on the red wine he usually took on Tuesday nights in preference to his customary beer. It was an innocent affirmation to all who knew him that he intended going for his regular weekly visit to Madame Culuhac's establishment later in the evening. Wine, he contended, was a help in such things.

Durand smiled up at two gentlemen who bowed and begged "a thousand pardons" as they squeezed through the narrow space toward a table further along the wall. He saw Flamart flick his forefinger to his eyebrow in a salute.

"The older one there, that's my boss, a nice fellow," the stone mason explained.

Durand nodded and then turned to press the debate with Montausier.

"Why don't we try to be more optimistic about human nature? Let's stop examining it so strictly and look on its faults with more indulgence."

"Indulgence," Montausier snorted through a smile he sought to repress. "Indulgence, ha! Indulgent Durand—the perfect description of our friend. And before you beam, it's no compliment."

"But in the world of today," Durand continued unruffled, "it is necessary to have a certain elasticity of virtue. Take your cherished virtue of wisdom, for example. It has to have the . . . the nice balance," he said, emphasizing his words with a gesture of his chunky hands. "Perfect reason, you know," he began the phrase from Molière that every schoolboy of his generation had learned, and went on to recite it almost as a jingle: "Perfect reason flees all extremity. It wishes one wise but with sobriety . . ."

"That's cheating and you know it." Montausier snapped, despising the adversary who would use catch phrases or invoke reverence for authority rather than argue the intrinsic merits of the question.

Flamart winced and glanced apologetically at his boss who viewed the argument from a nearby table.

"The great stiffness of the morality of the past is against the grain of our century and our usages," Durand persisted. "It demands too much perfection from mortals like us. And is there any greater folly than to stick one's nose into the business of correcting the world? Oh, I see, just as you do . . ."

"God," Montausier groaned with regret that Molière had ever been taught in that wretched lycée Durand once attended.

"No—me and Flamart here—we take mankind as it is, accustoming our souls to suffer what it does. And certainly our phlegm is as philosophic as your bile." Durand folded his hands over his paunch and watched Montausier reel under that blow. Let him find an answer to that. That, for example, was a coup to have made Aristotle proud.

"Well said," Flamart interjected solemnly, feeling that he should somehow join the conversation now that it included him.

"You add one fallacy to another," Montausier gasped. "Your reasoning is impertinent and dishonest. I won't discuss it further."

"Who won?" Durand asked, smiling at Flamart.

"I think you did."

"I'd rather lose than sink to that kind of reasoning." Montausier answered.

"Well, let's forget it," Durand said. He tactfully avoided Montausier's eyes and pretended to study posters advertising DUBONNET and MONTBAZILLAC and bus tours to Chartres.

Flamart sat directly beneath a life-size advertisement for "The Unfortunate One" opening at the Cine Olympia February 28. The star, Mademoiselle Edwige Desplaches, was pictured in tatters tied to a stake and surrounded by leering animals in a rear view that struck Durand as classically pathetic one moment and incredibly vulgar the next. She towered above Flamart's white hair in all of her grandly-but-tocked misery.

"Are you going to the movies tonight?" Montausier asked Durand.

"Yes, it's the Charlie Chaplin revival at the Cine Olympia," Durand said. "Care to come along?"

"No, I'm going to Madame Culuhac's with Flamart here. Why don't you come with us? This may be your last chance," Montausier said somberly.

"How's that?" Flamart blurted out. "Our last . . ."

"Oh, a bunch of women in the parish are starting a society to clean up the quarters. Father Trissotin mentioned it to me. They're out to protect youth from all forms of filth. You can be sure Madame Culuhac's place will be one of the targets. They'll be after you, too." he added to Durand.

The bookseller's heavy jowls sagged in astonishment. "Me? Why?"

"They always hit the bookshops, the art museums, the theatre, the whore houses—everything that's worthwhile." Montausier said. "My poor friend, you'll see. Groups who want the compulsory return of the Kingdom of God always attack books—anything that contains sex or ideas."

"Two of humanity's choicest commodities, just the same," Durand muttered.

"Agreed. But you'll see, my friend."

"They're going to close Madame Culuhac's?" Flamart

asked, as though he only now realized the full horror of Montausier's announcement.

"They'll certainly try to—and it won't be difficult to prove her Massage Parlor and Health Emporium is nothing but a bawdy house." He turned to Durand. "So, my friend, you'd better come and go with us."

"Sure—it's nice up there," Flamart said. "Why should they want to close such a . . ."

"Never," Durand said firmly. He indicated a repeat on the three glasses to the waiter. Then, seeing the crestfallen expression on Flamart's wrinkled face, he explained. "You know I never go to such places, my friend. It's against my code to have anything to do with professional women."

The stone mason blinked his total lack of understanding.

"He thinks it spoils it when you pay for it," Montausier added.

"Oh . . ." Flamart nodded vaguely.

"It's like bread, dear friend." Durand continued. "Some men like bought bread, and that's fine—but I prefer to bake my own."

"Only you don't always bake it at home," Flamart observed.

"Still, I bake it myself, rather than buy—don't you see? Why should I pay for what most of the women in Paris are happy to give me?"

"A stupid analogy," Montausier said. With bread at least you still buy the ingredients."

"And it's a lot more trouble," Flamart put in.

"I was just trying to make him understand," Durand said with some peevishness. "At least my way there's a sense of accomplishment—an art to it, let's say."

"Not meaning any reflection on you," Montausier hastened to reassure the stone mason.

The three men sat silent until the waiter returned with their glasses. Then Montausier lifted his beer in salute to Flamart and whispered reverently: "May God thee bless, if

Him it pleases."

And Durand, with equal reverence, supplied the second line of the couplet: "And guard thee well from social diseases."

Blood vessels in Flamart's tan cheeks reddened and a moist sentimentality brightened his eyes when he downed his wine to the toast honoring him. Truly, although the retired lawyer and the bookseller could be tedious and boring in their debates, they were the best companions the old man had ever had.

Silence gathered around them from the heaviness of dusk. Men glanced out to wintry twilight across the width of Boulevard St. Jacques. They saw the great oaks in the center promenade as nothing more than bleak, rain-illumined spectres.

3

Father Gregoire sat in the darkest corner of his cell and watched down-mistings of rain through his open windows.

From the corridor, the final movements of Schumann's *Waldscenen* filled the empty cells. It mollified for a moment the poverty and tawdriness of the old building as the great Alfred Cortot played another of his private concerts for the Dominican novices.

Father Gregoire, after greeting the pianist, had returned to his cell. No one could foresee when the prior might be called to the telephone or to see a visitor downstairs and he wanted no interruptions to mar his novices' enjoyment of the concert. Too, he preferred hearing the music alone in his semi-darkened cell rather than in the tiny, garishly lighted recreation room.

The cold scraped rawness up the monk's legs, but he did not move to close the window. He hunched forward on his massive bulk and rested his elbows on his knees while day moved slowly through its last grays toward night.

Lightning played silently over the rooftops of Paris. Father Gregoire listened to the hum of traffic on wet pavement and savored the subdued vitality of a great city closing itself into rooms for the night.

Now it was the jovial hunting portion of the *Waldscenen*—one of Father Gregoire's favorite passages in all music; a few measures of such felicity that he had once tried to learn them on the ancient upright player piano of the recreation room. When someone like Cortot played them, the monk never failed to feel himself returned to the universal order of things: of bathing and love and hunger and prayer and all the other elements of living. At such a time, it was good to sit in a monk's cell and view the world out there. He felt the rightness of humanity. It was good for a man to hurry from work to buy his bread, to have an aperitif at the cafe with his friends, to stop and buy his newspaper at one of the kiosks, to step into the public urinal down there on the corner and piss, then to go home, to read his paper, to eat, to rest, to hold the bodies of his wife and children in his glance or in his arms; and good to argue and shave and make love within the walls of the small portion of a city that was his home.

It was the same over and over again. Every night men returned home, every night it was the same and every night it was new.

And in the cloister every evening was the same and every evening was new. Dusk changed the texture of walls and floors within a cell as it changed the texture of solitude and prayers. At dusk a man behind monastery walls entered deeply either into love or into loneliness.

Father allowed himself to be caught up without resistance in the permeation of music combining with twilight. He did not look up when footsteps, accompanied by rustle of heavy robes, passed his open door and entered the cubicle a few feet beyond at the end of the hall. He heard the latch slide cautiously against the music. Absently, Father waited to hear the flushing from the cubicle. Instead he heard a paroxysm of coughing. He told himself it was Friar Lupe, gone there to have his spell so that no more noise than necessary would disturb the novices' enjoyment of Cortot's recital. Father judged the young Spanish friar must have his head out the open window, for he heard the coughing more clearly through his cell window than from under the cubicle door.

The music came to a halt. Muffled applause clattered through the hall.

Father Gregoire rose heavily and walked into the black hole of the corridor. He must go thank Cortot for the recital. He hesitated. To his right, from the cubicle, Father Lupe's coughing rose to an almost unbearable climax.

The prior rapped lightly at the door with the back of his hand.

"Are you all right, Lupe?"

A gasped "Yes, Father" preceded another deep-chested cough that reverberated through the now silent building.

4

The coughing drifted downward to the ears of Charles Durand as he rounded the corner from Boulevard St. Jacques and began the steep ascent of the Street of the Seven Angels.

"Cough it up," the bookseller murmured pleasantly to the deserted street. He stopped and peered about to locate the sound. It floated to him directionless, diffused through the mutter of rain on the dome of his umbrella.

Did it come from Mademoiselle Mailleferre's shuttered apartment there to his left over the Religious Art Shop? Not unless she had a man up there, and one could imagine Madame Culuhac's entertaining the League of Purity far easier than Mademoiselle Mailleferre's entertaining a man in her living quarters. Poor skinny bitch, Durand mused, had she ever had her little needle threaded? She stood out as the only woman Durand had ever met who elicited absolutely no response in him. The fact that she did nothing to his paunch gave Durand an illusion of purity around her that he occasionally liked to experience.

No, there was the cough again, from the house of sanctity here to his right. He should have guessed immediately. Lonely coughs always went with such places. What else was there for a poor bastard to do in there? Pray and cough.

The thought filled Durand with a certain nostalgia which he tried to dispel by studying chalked obscenities diluted in down-dribblings of rain on the cloister walls. He waddled leisurely up the cobblestone incline beside the hideous red brick building. Such a place. These monks lived in extreme poverty in the center of the world's capital of pleasure.

Durand hesitated at the entrance door, painted green and pealing now. Its brass plaque identified the address as number 5. He glanced around the empty street, then opened the door and stuck his head in. An odor of cold incense floated to him from the chapel to the right of the hall; it mingled with the reek of cabbage and onions from the kitchen. Durand smiled at the fine thought of something pointedly significant in this juxtaposition of incense and cabbage—symbols of man's natural and supernatural life. He would think it out and then condense it into one of his epigrams and toss it off some afternoon at the cafe. This would put old Montausier in a proper rage, for although the retired lawyer never ceased harping on the faults of the clergy, he held the Dominicans in high esteem.

A rumble of footsteps on the stair attracted Durand's attention toward the far right rear of the entrance hall. He saw a skeletal, white-haired layman, wrapped in an overcoat and scarf, accompanied by a large monk in white robes, his graying hair cut in that ridiculous Dominican tonsure as a circle around his head.

"I can't tell you what this kindness means to us here," the monk's deep voice echoed down the hall. "May I call you a cab?"

"Please."

"Fine. If you'll take a seat here in the parlor. . . ."

Durand quietly withdrew, closing the door. When he turned back to the street, lights had popped noiselessly on. A line of yellow street lamps curved upward, each a dot of brightness surrounded by its halo of mist. Near the top of the hill, past the tobacco shop and the Breville Museum, he saw the hazed neon lettering of Madame Culuhac's sign. It shone only as a red blear through the rain, but Durand knew what it said. Did he not notice it a thousand times a day from his bookshop display window across the street?

RELAXING MASSAGE

And everyone in the quarter knew what that meant. Such a neighborhood, really. A man didn't have to leave this narrow, winding street to get anything he wanted.

Yes, starting here on this side he could get a prayer at the Dominicans, then tobacco next door at Madame Carnot's, then edification at the Breville Museum, then a screwing at Madame Culuhac's, then justice around the bend at the *Palais de Justice*, or the time of day from the clock tower above it. And he needed only to cross the street and return toward the boulevard to get a haircut at the barber's, a book at Durand's, shoes, clothes, insurance and spices at other shops, a rosary or a religious calendar at Mademoiselle Mailleferre's, or dwelling in any of the second or third floor apartments that appeared to lean out over the narrow street above the shops. All of man's physical and spiritual needs could be handled right there.

Durand realized, with astonished delight, that he was on the side of the spiritual, supplying the quarter with books.

A flash of lightning pinpointed in greenish focus the glistening cobblestones and lamp posts and shuttered windows. Instantly the electricity on this side of Boulevard St. Jacques blacked out.

5

Hell.

Madame Culuhac jiggled the light switch and cursed in a voice tempered to dignity by years of practice in the discreet discussion of indiscretions with men—a matronly voice with distinguished overtones.

Damn. With the lights knocked out, she would have to send the girls into the streets to solicit. Never a satisfactory idea. You could count on it most of them would cheat on you once they got out of your sight.

She walked heavily to the window across the room, separated the lace curtains with her hands and peered out. A faint odor of dust detached from the lace. The streets three stories below were black all the way to the boulevard. From the Cine Olympia on the other side of the boulevard, the sky glowed red each time the neon movie sign flickered on and faded to black each time it flickered off. Madame watched the reddish blear, silhouetting rooftops, come and go.

She stood at the third-story window and thought of Albert, rest him, and how it would have hurt him to see the wretched way things had come to pass. The new world, the post-war world, the Christian world was upon them in Paris, of all places. The old amiability was fast disappearing.

Father Gregoire fumbled his way along the corridor toward his cell. Door facings and sweating expanses of wall chilled his fingertips.

Others moved in the darkness. Footsteps clumped, robes

rustled and light switches clicked.

"No need to try the lights," he announced to the darkness. "The electricity seems to be off all over the quarter.

A crash shook the floor. All other movement abruptly halted. Father Gregoire's sense of orientation leaped back into focus as he listened to the low moan from the toilet cubicle at the end of the hall. He hurried forward, guided by his concentration on the boy. An invisible mass slowed him directly in front of the door. His hand searched forward, found the knob and pulled. The door held. Vaguely he remembered having heard Lupe latch it from inside.

"Lupe . . ." he said quietly, his mouth so close to the door he smelled his echoing breath, warm and fragrant with the ferment of this morning's communion wine. "Are you hurt?"

Through the wood he heard a sloughing movement, as though the boy were struggling to get up, and then the thump of his head hard against the floor.

Father Gregoire felt himself wince. "Bring candles," he called quietly into the darkness.

Footsteps approached from the cell across the hall.

"Is that you, Marie-Martin?"

"Yes," the monk said. "What's happened?"

"Call the doctor. It's Lupe."

Gregoire heard the priest walk away. He turned back to the door where his hand still warmed the black knob. "Lupe, can you reach the latch? Try to open it."

Silence. Close by the rain poured and wind rushed under the door, around Father's feet. Lupe must have left the cubicle window open, he reasoned. He was probably lying there getting soaked.

One of the novices hastened down the corridor with a candle. In its troubled circle of light his eyes shown with concern.

The prior gripped the door knob with both hands, braced his right foot against the door facing, pulling slowly until the wood splintered and the door swung open. He looked down through inpouring slants of candlelit rain. Lupe lay sprawled on the floor with his head twisted at an odd angle against the commode.

Father Gregoire bent and lifted the white bundle easily in his arms. Odors of wet cloth that bore faint traces of mothballs filled his nostrils. The novice who held the candle stepped quickly into the cubicle and closed the window, modulating the rain to a rumble against glass.

Preceded by the candle-bearer, the monk carried Lupe down the hall and lowered him onto his cot.

"Get blankets," he said. "All the blankets you can find."

The novice left the candle on Lupe's bedside table and hurried from the room. Father placed his hand on Lupe's moist cheek. Beneath the cold surface of the flesh, he felt the heat of fever. One side of the boy's head glistened wet from the rain. Father Gregoire stripped him of his damp clothes and used them as a wad to rough dry the friar's hair. The thinness of the youth's brown arms and legs, all muscle and bone, and the skeletal chest alarmed the prior. He promised himself to see that Lupe got supplementary food and that he ate it. He pulled Lupe's blanket over him and tucked it under the boy's body.

The novice returned with three more blankets in his arms. Father guessed he must have jerked them from the beds of other novices, since they were in disarray.

When the two covered Lupe, the novice stood back and awaited further instructions.

"Go to the front door. Wait for the doctor and bring him here immediately."

Gregoire pulled Lupe's straight-back chair to the cot and sat down to wait. The friar looked terribly young in the candlelight, scarcely more than a child despite his nineteen years. Father noted the smoothness of his face, the look of health that sickness brought.

Lupe's lips moved. Gregoire bent forward to hear. A paroxysm convulsed the boy's chest and filled his mouth. The monk lifted the friar's head and pressed a drinking glass to the corner of his lips. A thick blackish fluid half-filled the glass. The boy's eyes opened and rolled upward to see the priest. They filled with abject apology. When he had finished, Gregoire placed the glass on the floor, wiped Lupe's mouth with an edge of blanket and lowered his head back to the pillow.

"I'm sorry, Father," Lupe mumbled. The words formed a pink bubble at the corner of his lips which immediately burst. He closed his eyes again.

"That's all right, Lupe. Just lie quietly. You'll be all right."

The youth's teeth clenched and his face darkened against the candlelit whiteness of his pillow. A struggle started deep within him.

Father Gregoire bent forward, reached under the blankets and rested his large hand lightly on Lupe's burning chest. With each intake of breath, the chest cavity quavered against the priest's palm.

The candle spat at his elbow. Father wondered at the silence that had settled through the old building, as though he and the boy were left alone in the rainy night.

He looked at Lupe's black sputum-stained lips. Odors of age and dampness from the surrounding walls mingled with the reek of cabbages and onions from the kitchen below. A bell rang downstairs, calling the community to before-supper prayers in the chapel. The monk rubbed his free hand over his cheek and felt the evening stubble and the skin oils. He became aware of his bulk beneath the heavy white robe, of the taste in his mouth, and the health of his belly. With the sudden certainty that Lupe was dying, the grossness of his own animal well-being blared at him.

He sat heavy in the cell's flickering light and listened through the palm of his hand to the sickness within the friar's chest.

7

Durand felt his way along the darkened street, mightily pleased with his free night away from home. He turned in at the tobacco shop where candlelight shone dimly through the red checkered curtain at the glassed upper portion of the door.

"*Bonsoir*, Madame Carnot," he said to the accompaniment of the door's tinkling bell.

"Monsieur Durand," the proprietress said with amiable dignity.

"A pack of Bleues for myself," he said, putting his umbrella in the rack near the door. "And a pack of Players for my wife, and . . ."

"She is learning to like the English brand, your wife," Madame Carnot said as she placed two packs of cigarettes on the flickering glass counter and watched Durand approach.

"Yes, they are milder and . . ."

"Oh, the Turkish tobacco is far superior, really."

"Or is it Egyptian, Madame?"

"Now, I am confused. In any case, the one is . . ."

Lightning crashed into the street outside, rattling windows and shelves. It blinded them for a moment.

"My God!" Madame Carnot cried.

"Ah . . . that was close," Durand said in awe.

"Why, it was frightening! We could have been killed."

Madame Carnot calmed and withdrew her hand from Durand's warm grasp in that awkwardness that seeks above all not to offend a good client and at the same time to maintain a semblance of propriety in order not to appear forward with someone about whose intimate taste and morals one is uncertain. Obviously with those full cheeks and jovial eyes this man was not fanatically chaste, but then again, despite the awful rumors about him, he did appear to be thoughtful and devot-

ed husband; and did he not regularly purchase the pious little
quarterly called *Conjugal Spirituality*? Who could tell? In any
case, his paunch was not that of an ascetic, of that she was certain. She felt his forefinger tickle against her palm when she
withdrew her hand, and involuntarily she gave an answering
tickle before falling into confusion.

"M'sieu! . . ."

"Only a jest, Madame," he laughed. "Can you blame me
if a handsome woman puts her hand in mine in a moment of
distress and nature momentarily overcomes good breeding?"

"You flatter me," she smiled in the cramped and one-
sided way that would permit him to see the candlelight on the
gold tooth in her lower left jaw. "But you do not deceive me.
Middle-aged men look to youth for their follies, not to the elderly."

"Ah, but there you make the common mistake of stereo-
typing us," Durand smiled. He leaned forward and crossed his
arms on the counter. "Each differs according to his own deter-
mination and not according to some predetermination," he
said expansively.

Madame Carnot forgot the gold tooth and her usually
pursed smile spread to one of open admiration.

"M'sieu—you are in the vein tonight, but . . ."

"I will not hide from you, Madame, that you have long
attracted me."

He looked down toward his hands and then glanced up
into her face over the metal rims of his glasses.

"Otherwise why should I stop in here every night to make
my little purchases of tobacco and pencil leads?" he added,
pleased with this implication that when her charm ceased, his
patronage would cease. This element of insidious threat was so
spontaneous that Durand could only consider it an inspiration, a positive inspiration that altered the tone of the flirtation by placing him in that splendidly brutal category of the
old feudal barons who threatened to oust aged fathers from
their tenants lands unless daughters acceded to their lecherous

whims. This was only a tiny such thing, of course, but it had overtones of male domination that enchanted Durand.

"It is not entirely one-sided," Madame Carnot fenced. "I can say now that I look forward to the most banal of your visits with anticipation. But then, we are not irresponsible children. I have my old man, and you have your own obligations, have you not?"

"Madame will forgive me," Durand said resignedly.

"May heaven forgive us both for this momentary madness, and give us the strength, M'sieu," she nodded, "the necessary strength. . . ."

The opening door caused Durand to straighten up. At least the old bitch was stringing along, he thought; her last statement indicated she wanted the flirtation to continue.

A heavyset young woman stamped water from her galoshes at the door and called out: "A package of Bleues, love?" Her vapid glance settled on Durand and turned seductive.

"Well, hello everybody. . . . Foul weather, eh? But nice for some things though . . ." she said looking into Durand's eyes.

He bowed stiffly and did not answer.

"Correct change," she said, spilling coins on the counter. "Thank you, love." She winked at Madame Carnot and walked with strange lightness for her weight out the front door.

Durand snorted with disgust.

"I guess you showed her," Madame Carnot said. "You were admirable, entirely admirable."

"One of Madame Culuhac's pigeons, I suppose," Durand muttered. "Don't believe I've seen her on the streets before."

"Ah yes. She's a new one. Honestly, I wish they would take their business elsewhere, but what can I . . ."

"You are not responsible for the morals of your clients." he said. "Don't worry—scum like that will come to their proper reward in hell."

"Ah, that! How right you are."

Madame Carnot began wrapping his cigarettes. She

turned her head to the side and eyed him over the candle's flame. "You were admirable, bowing politely like that. I guess that made her feel cheap enough."

In the intimate light, silence settled warm between them. Durand leaned on the scratched glass counter-top again and listened to the faint sizzle of the radiator to one side, and the steady downpour beyond the closed front door.

"About women like that," Durand whispered.

"Vultures, that's what they are. Pardon, you were saying?"

"I was only going to say," he mumbled self-consciously, "that although I've not led a blameless life, I . . ."

"After all, you're human, M'sieu. And from what I gather, a man in his prime," she encouraged, her bony hands at rest on the partially wrapped package.

"Yes—human enough," he said. "And perhaps weak in my affections—too susceptible to certain temptations. . . ."

"And what one of God's poor creatures isn't, occasionally?"

"Still, I can tell you in confidence—and without meaning to sound pretentious—that I have never had recourse to such creatures as that. Not once in my fifty-three years."

"I revere you for it—believe me," she nodded to emphasize her feelings. "Few men can make such a statement, I feel sure."

Durand smelled the candle's nearness and felt its faint warmth on his cheek. He hesitated, attempting to decide which of the two pleasures to pursue: the flirtation, to this equally gratifying one of drawing Madame Carnot into that other type of sensuality; or the self-righteous one wherein two people share their virtue. But the flirtation would last much longer and be more savory with its advances and retards, particularly since they had managed to create an atmosphere in which both were committed to the wonderful complexity of trying to resist it.

Paper crackled the silence as Madame Carnot resumed wrapping. Durand mentioned that since his mother-in-law was coming for her regular Tuesday night visit, he was on his way to his regular Tuesday night movie.

"It's the Charlie Chaplin revival," he said. If you'd care to come with me? Or am I being offensive again?"

"I do wish I could, M'sieu. But you know it's impossible."

Durand shook his head understandingly and handed her a bill. From the change he left his customary small tip on the counter. Madame Carnot vacillated between the business and the niceties of her romance. She glanced at his paunch, bulging under his vest at the opening of his overcoat in a majestic curve from chest of groin, and at the neat center in his thinning hair that gave such a noble impression of breadth to his forehead. She handed the coin back and begged him not to cheapen their relationship with any further such gratuities.

"Ah, that lightning. I do hope it doesn't strike again," she said.

"Would you like me to stay with you until the electricity comes back on?" Durand suggested.

"Others will be coming in, M'sieu. It might look—you know."

Durand chuckled and laid his hand over hers. He felt its icy tender thinness and told himself that she was emotionally torn up by his presence. He might even successfully force the issue, crude as that was. But no, that would end it in consummation and deprive them of the deeper connoisseur's pleasure of a gradual seduction. She glanced toward the window and did not draw her hand from his.

"How is it that we can feel so guilty and worry about what others think when we have done nothing—though I confess I am thinking things that would cause you to slap my face at this moment." He burst into full laughter that somewhat affronted Madame Carnot and made her wonder what crudeness lay in that paunch. However, though she felt disappointment that he did not take a more delicate and sighing approach, she managed to laugh with him and assured him that lightning was never supposed to strike twice in the same place.

"Right now," she added demurely, "I'd feel safer with you gone."

"You probably would be," he agreed.

"What?"

"Safer with me gone. . . . Ah me, men are strange and pathetic creatures," he said pensively.

"Women, too, M'sieu."

He sighed. "We think that when we marry, this will solve all our temptations. Then we meet some woman—a spark flies—something stirs inside. We're pitifully torn in our affections."

"It's the same for us, M'sieu."

"And it seems that passion stays strong with the passing of years—perhaps even grows stronger. . . ."

"Yes," she nodded.

Durand detected candle light glistening brighter at the under-rims of Madame Carnot's eyes and was glad to see he had brought the soft mood of tears on her.

"Well, I must go . . ." he said.

"Yes. . . ." She stared down at her hands, working with her fingernails.

"Good night, Madame," he said tenderly from door.

"Good night, M'sieu. . . ."

The whore walked carefully along the street. That fat jowled sonofabitch back there bowing at her like that. She could've slapped his face. Who was he trying to impress—that old crone who ran the place? The big hypocrite.

The cinemas across the boulevard would soon open. Her galoshes pulled at the wet cobblestones. Below, at the end of the street, she saw cars pass along the boulevard, their head-lights reflecting jagged streaks beneath them. Spasmodic coughing floated to her from somewhere behind the wall to her left, made distant by the gurgle of invisible water in the gutter beside her. She ambled toward the boulevard's points of light.

"Dear Friends," Mademoiselle Mailleferre apologized. "How could I have been so stupid as to make no provision for candles in such an eventuality?"

Murmured reassurances sprang to her from the darkness of her parlor. She was not stupid at all. Who could foresee that the electricity would go out?

From the counterpoint of soprano voices, Father Trissotin's bass detached itself with sonorous masculinity. "It is in darkness that man sometimes accomplishes the most rewarding of his goals," he said.

To Mesdames Ponneger and Duric, widows, and to Mesdames Hilhaud and Aurey, married, the priest's fine phrase evoked the most regrettable suggestiveness. They were glad for the dark that hid their scandalized expressions, and each sought to find less obvious and more spiritual meanings in Father Trissotin's pleasantly cryptic remark.

To Mademoiselles Toulenc and Mailleferre, spinsters of the type Father Trissotin thought militantly virginal, his remark was ghastly and they sought to rise above it in a sort of mental purging at which they had long since become adept.

"We cannot very well continue the meeting, dear friends, until there are lights so the secretary can take her notes," Mademoiselle Mailleferre said with reserve. "So what shall we do? Father, would you care to use this moment to deliver the little homily you have for us tonight?"

"My dear Mademoiselle," the priest's voice boomed out.

"I am granted only the ordinary gifts of the sacerdote—not those extraordinary ones of divination and blind sight. I must have lights to read my little notes."

Laughter enlivened the darkness at this fine phrase which erased the former cryptic one.

"May I say something?" Madame Ponneger asked as though the answer were obvious.

"Of course."

"Well, I tell you, Dear Friends, since I have already been placed in charge of the film division of our *Société* or whatever we are to call ourselves, I should like to get on with my tasks as quickly as possible. Tonight is the last night of the Charlie Chaplin Revival at the Cine Olympia, and I think I should observe that film, don't you?"

"I certainly do," Father Trissotin said.

"So, can't we hurry on with the meeting even in the darkness?"

"Very well," Mademoiselle Mailleferre assented. "Where were we?"

"I believe we were preparing to vote on a name for the group when the lights went out," Father Trissotin prompted. "Someone suggested that you call yourselves simply "Groupe des six." I feel that although this is an original enough name, you automatically delimit yourselves from future recruits by adopting such a title."

"Well, that makes sense," Madame Ponneger said.

"I was thinking, if you'll let me interject here," Madame Aurey said in her careful and precise manner of enunciating every syllable, "of something like 'The Waverly Group.' I know it's not French, but it does sound distinguished."

"Well, what's it supposed to signify?" Madame Ponneger asked.

"Nothing really. A friend from England sent me a box of the most beautiful and distinctive stationary. It was Waverly Fine Papers. The name has always intrigued me. How about 'The Waverly Anti-Pornographic Society'?"

"Now, I am only your advisor, your coadjutor," Father Trissotin interrupted, "and the final decisions are, of course, up to you. But I suggest you call yourselves something like *The Société for the Preservation of Christian Morality Against Contemporary Indecency,* St. Jacques Parish District Division." Father Trissotin waited in silence for some note of approval.

"It seems a bit long," Madame Duric said apologetically.

"It would cost a fortune to get that much title printed on our letterheads." Madame Ponneger put in.

"Very well," Father's laughter resounded in the dark. "I certainly don't want to impose my wishes."

"I didn't mean to imply that, Father," Madame Duric hastened to reassure him. "I was only thinking out loud for a moment—I meant it only as a suggestion."

"Of course. Well, when you asked me to be your coadjutor, I gave this a lot of thought and . . ."

"What about something colorful like Daughters of the King? I was thinking of that," Madame Ponneger interrupted as though the matter were settled for all time.

"*Les filles du Roi,*" Mademoiselle Toulenc mused. "I think it's charming."

"Couldn't it be construed as royalist?" Madame Duric suggested.

"The royalty of God." Madame Ponneger snapped defensively. "What's wrong with that kind of royalty, I'd like to know?"

"In any case, dear friends," Father said loudly above the babbling. "One moment, please ladies. In any case, I believe there is an organization of Protestant women who call themselves Daughters of the King.

"Well, that lets that out." Madame Ponneger grunted.

"I think we should consider the title you suggested, Father, and pass on for the moment to other things," Mademoiselle Mailleferre said.

"Well, I would like to make a point," Father Trissotin

said, "that we should be open and above board about this thing from the very outset. Beginnings are so important you know. I am convinced there should be no secret handshakes or passwords as has been suggested. Now, you have a lot of groundwork to cover at this first meeting, so if you'll permit me, I'll make a few more suggestions."

"Go right ahead, Father," Madame Ponneger said in a voice that made the priest nostalgic for his father. "And let me say that you are doing all right without your notes."

When the laughter at this fine phrase had died down, Father Trissotin, relieved that Madame Ponneger had got over her pique so quickly, resumed. "So far then, subject of course to your approval, we have a name and I believe that we decided on the motto: "Freedom from Filth in the St. Jacques Paris District!" since we hope other responsible women from other parishes all over Paris will follow your example and join in this crusade with you."

"I think this thrilling," Madame Aurey said.

"It is," Madame Ponneger affirmed.

"Now there is one thing I feel I must say," Father Trissotin observed, his voice shifting into a lower register of intense seriousness. "Let me be frank. Our goal is an atmosphere cleansed of filth in which to bring up the children of this parish. We are all adult human beings. What we are combating is evil and ugly and dirty—and could certainly be embarrassing to persons of your refinement. But remember this important point. It is not what you know that harms you, but what you love. Think about that for a moment. Since all of us loathe these things, then the knowledge and free discussion of them will not harm us, for we are bringing them up to our level. Therefore, we must not be embarrassed by the sordid details that will arise, but must treat them boldly and dynamically. Some of us will be obliged to see and hear and read some shockingly vile things—things that you perhaps never knew existed. It will take a truly militant Christian spirit of courage to expose yourselves to such salacious and really shocking things. But never forget that you are doing it as a doctor who delves into filth to bring forth health. With that attitude, you will find the fortitude to suffer through the oceans of filth to which you will be exposed in order to bring our children to health in an atmosphere uncontaminated."

"Well, I never heard that point explained quite so beautifully," Madame Duric said. The others agreed, their voices quiet with emotion.

"It's very moving, really," Mademoiselle Mailleferre said huskily.

"Thank you." Father replied. "Now, in my opinion, since we are few and the objectives are great, we must divide ourselves into basic sections, such as the very important Film Division of which we have already voted Madame Ponneger the chairman and sole member. Other suggestions that will serve a critical need at this point, and my suggestions for their chairmanships are:

"First, we need a Public Park and Museum Division. All of us know about the lewd markings penciled on so many of the statues and . . ."

"Not only are the markings on the statues lewd, but most of the statues themselves are too," Mademoiselle Toulenc put in.

"Nearly all of them are," Madame Ponneger added. "That *Reclining Diana* over at the museum is about the lewdest thing I ever saw—all sprawled out there naked as the day she was born. Did you ever see such a thing, Father?"

The silence grew nettles. Mademoiselle Mailleferre felt herself cramp into a tighter space in the dark. It seemed to her, and she felt the others must sense it too, that the detailed marble pudenda of that *Reclining Diana* floated about the room like some luminous phantom. Father Trissotin had certainly seen the statue, and the way she lay spread-eagle, her "shameful parts" literally slapped you in the face. That blabbermouth Ponneger would have to bring everyone's attention to the fact that Father had seen it, and set everyone's imagination fulminating. One simply did not place a priest in such an embarrassing situation. She searched for something to say, something to relieve the terrible silence.

"This is where we have a delicate problem," Father Trissotin said in a voice that indicated he had lost none of the innuendo and was pained. "I agree, of course, that many of these statues are frankly disgusting. But we have to act wisely, and I do not think we can attack the actual statues. Some of them are classic works, you know, and . . ."

"Is that *Reclining Diana* supposed to be a classic work?" Madame Ponneger asked sharply.

Mademoiselle Mailleferre wondered at the woman's brass. One would think, after making such a blunder as she had just made, she would not open her mouth for the rest of the evening.

"I'm sure it's considered a classic work," Father answered.

"What? I would like to know," Madame Aurey asked, choosing her words carefully, "is what there is about a classic work that makes it any less lewd than another? Can someone tell me that? What has its *classicality* got to do with that?"

"That's what I'd like to know," Madame Ponneger challenged.

"It's a very difficult problem."

"Would you want one of your altar boys to look at a thing like that?" Madame Ponneger asked.

"Of course not. But you must remember that these are the artistic expressions of another age—a sort of history of their times, and as such have a certain value. Most of these pieces date from the Greek and Roman eras."

"I think one must distinguish between whether a thing is great art or not," Mademoiselle Mailleferre suggested, "especially ancient things."

"I might remind you," Madame Aurey said primly, "of Michelangelo's *David*. You'd have to look far to find anything more obscene than that. And it certainly is not from the Greek and Roman eras."

Mademoiselle Mailleferre's inner vision saw again that disturbing statue in all its traumatic clarity, the marble-veined buttocks so hauntingly beautiful and so distressing, the genitals darkened by the touches of how many curious hands. . . . Could such a ravishing thing really be—

Madame Ponneger's coarse voice interrupted her revery. "I don't discriminate between nude bodies—whether or not they are artistic expressions. It's all lustful to me."

Madame Ponneger's arrogance aroused in Mademoiselle Mailleferre the desire to rise to the *David's* defense, even though the statue had caused her such unhappiness through the years.

"But we must realize that these statues do come from past ages," Father Trissotin asserted. "To us, with our greater spiritual refinement, many of them are frankly disgusting, I wholly agree. But so-called specialists—among them some of our own clergy and hierarchy—insist that they are masterpieces and that we . . ."

"Are the Dominicans especially that way, Father?" Madame Aurey asked. "My son brought me some of the works of Father de Vann, and he just comes out and says that although masterpieces of art may not save the soul, they make the soul worth saving."

A murmur of distaste ran through the room. Mademoiselle Mailleferre thought of the Dominicans across the street. Their coarseness of appearance had always offended her. She felt sure any one of them would be capable of making just such an obtuse statement.

"Well, Father de Vanne's a Thomist," Father Trissotin explained. "You can't do much with those people."

"How about the Jesuits?" Mademoiselle Toulenc asked. I understand they're much more narrow-minded . . . I mean much stricter in their interpretation of theology."

"I'm afraid some of them also share a high regard for this sort of thing. In any case, we must restrain ourselves from any concerted efforts to have these statues removed or destroyed.

The press can quickly make such things appear absurd, and we don't want that."

"In the meantime, I suppose we must allow them to go on perverting our youth," Madame Ponneger said. "I thought this was to be a group for . . ."

"Indeed, I admit my own astonishment at this fact," Father Trissotin said with some liveliness. "I am, as you know, somewhat of a specialist in the problems of youth. I have never heard of a single instance where statues like these had anything to do with sins or crimes committed. The *markings* on them, yes. But strangely the statues do not apparently incite our youth to impurities as much as one might imagine."

"What about the old men?" Madame Ponneger called out. "There's everlastingly a crowd of them hanging around gawking at that *Reclining Diana*."

Mademoiselle Mailleferre wondered what business took Madame Ponneger so often to Breville Museum. She apparently knew a great deal of what went on there.

"For the moment, let's leave the statues," Father Trissotin pleaded. "Our first concern is our youth. Let's appoint or elect what we might call a guardian—someone who will station herself unobtrusively behind bushes in the park or behind drapes in the museum and bring charges, in the name of the *Société* against anyone caught making lascivious markings on these pieces of so-called art. I suggest Madame Hilhaud, since she is married and can ask her husband's advice and help in the event anything truly noxious should come up."

"Then, of course," he continued, "in any such crusade there should be a Pledge of Purity Division, one of you—I suggest Mademoiselle Mailleferre as ideal for this—would make calls throughout the parish and seek to get entire families to sign these pledges."

Silence, full of constraint, followed for a long moment.

"Such pledges of course do not infringe upon marital rights in any way," Father explained, and the silence became less strained.

"Father, I'm not meaning to question the wisdom of this in any way," Madame Aurey said. "But I've been given to understand that many priests are against such practices . . . ."

"Father de Vannes, again, I suppose. . ."

"No, my husband read an article condemning them as Jansenistic and puritanical not too long ago."

"Where did he read this?" Father Trissotin asked with impatience.

"I'm sure it was in *Happy Foyers.*"

"I see. A fine magazine. Certainly, however, it all depends on how you handle it. After all, we're not asking anything that is not normal and human and Christian. As I said, marital rights are undisturbed. Admittedly there's a degree of fanaticism among certain of those Jansenistic men, but that should not mean condemnation of the good parts of their doctrine, now should it?"

"I don't see anything fanatic about it at all," Madame Ponneger said.

"I think it could be a great help," Mademoiselle Mailleferre agreed. "Particularly to the young. There's something about pledging yourself that strengthens the will, isn't there, Father?"

"There certainly is. Now, let's get on. We need a Decent Literature Division to discourage and condemn some of this flow of really unspeakable material that is openly sold today. This has been tried with great success in America, Ireland and England. One of you, with my help, will draw up a list of objectionable books and then go around to the bookstores and request that they remove them from their shelves."

"I could give you a list already," Madame Ponneger said. "What about Rabelais and Balzac, for example?"

"And Huysmans?" Mademoiselle Mailleferre added.

"Molière and Racine . . ."

"Here again we have the same problem as we did with the statues," Father said regretfully.

"The problems of what is classical again, I suppose," Madame Duric sighed.

"Yes—all of these works have established reputations as serious contributions to literature. We may as well face it. In this fallen day and age there is a certain rabid element who make a sort of religion of art, who think it is sacrosanct, untouchable. If we attack so-called respectable works, we will be defeated at the outset by public opinion. We must begin with the newer works, those that have not established literary reputations. Many of them contain passages or words capable of influencing our youth to immoral desires or acts. And then, only when we have expanded our prestige and gained experience can we bring pressures for the suppression of such works as those of Rabelais, Balzac, Maupassant, Flaubert and so forth."

"I feel like we're in the beginning of something terribly important," Madame Aurey whispered to Mademoiselle Mailleferre.

"It's such a challenge," Mademoiselle Mailleferre answered.

"I suggest that Madame Duric could head this division," Father Trissotin continued.

"I'm to make a list of objectionable books and ask the bookshops to stop selling them?"

"That's right. Explain why we want these works removed."

"Father," Mademoiselle Mailleferre said, "do you really think someone like Durand will comply? He's not even a Christian."

"I don't know him very well . . ."

"Well, we all know his wife and mother-in-law," Madame Duric said.

"Wonderful Christian women," Father observed.

"His wife's a little strange, though. Had you noticed? She doesn't mix with people much. Never joins any of the groups."

"She's probably embarrassed that her husband's not of

the Faith."

"Perhaps if we talked to her and her mother, they might persuade Durand to comply."

"Well, I'll tell you," Father Trissotin said slowly. "There are ways and there are ways. Now, you just tell Durand and the other booksellers that if they cooperate, we will urge our parishioners to patronize their stores, and that if they do not, we will simply put their names on our parish bulletin as refusing to cooperate with us in our attempts to preserve our children from filth. He'll get the message all right. With such threats of boycott and public censure, most booksellers, you can bet, will come into line quickly enough," he chuckled. "They may pretend to be champions of literature, but when the profits stop coming in, they'll change their tune."

Shouldn't we have opened this meeting with some sort of prayer?" Madame Ponneger suddenly asked.

"We did, my dear," Mademoiselle Mailleferre answered frostily. "You arrived after we'd finished." The idea that anything would begin without a prayer in her household struck Mademoiselle Mailleferre as an insult.

"Now we come to the last and certainly one of the most important divisions," Father Trissotin said. "But one that will require the assistance of your husbands and sons. So I think Madame Aurey should be placed in charge of the Division For the Distribution of Religious Pamphlets in Public Men's Rooms. Her husband and son can report to her and handle the actual distribution. It's no secret that the walls of such places are covered with pornographic drawings and writings. It is especially necessary to provide religious pamphlets so that men will have something edifying to read rather than allow their attention to go to the wall writings."

Mesdames Hilhaud and Aurey began chattering about the stupendously vulgar things their husbands said were written in such places. Madame Hilhaud, on this score, recommended that the *Société* also study the ethics of whether or not those female attendants, no matter how old and decrepit they were, should not be barred from working in the men's side of public rest rooms. "Certainly, there are plenty of impoverished old men who could take up the cause and unlock the doors on the men's side."

"It must be sickening to be a man and to have to go into such places at all," Mademoiselle Mailleferre moaned. "How can you, a priest of God, bear it, Father?"

Darkness became luminous with the shock of her indiscretion. Mademoiselle wrung her hands, despising herself and feeling that all others despised her for intimating in this tactless way that their spiritual director could stoop to reading the wall writing or lusting after the hags who unlocked the cubicle doors. She realized that her clumsiness was even worse than Madame Ponneger's. She told herself that she was overly tired and therefore not responsible. But self-loathing sickened her. Never would she have ever dreamed she could be so lacking in tact.

Then a knuckle-joint popped in the silence as all worked their minds to find some words, some subject that would cover the embarrassment and send the conversation to more elevated ground.

"I vote that we accept all of Father Trissotin's suggestions by affirmation in block," Mademoiselle Toulence finally blurted out.

"Aye!" Madame Ponneger voted.

"My dear," Mademoiselle Mailleferre said in a voice of tremulous self-reproach. "I think we move to do such things, not vote."

"That is correct," Father Trissotin affirmed with clipped and defensive accents of utter gentleness which implied that he fully forgave Mademoiselle Mailleferre, but would nevertheless prefer to be spared any further public allusions to his functions or his morals.

"Second the motion!" Madame Ponneger said desperately.

The electricity flared up. Mademoiselle Mailleferre, her throat still mottled with the flush of her unfortunate blunder, reached across a tray of assorted tarts and cookies for her notebook to begin jotting down the minutes of this important first meeting. But the bulb faded again, slowly resolving the room into grayness and then blackness.

10

Hell.

Madame Culuhac jerked the bead cord of her lamp but the briefly-returned electricity was gone. Well, it wouldn't do any good to have the lights on now anyway with the girls already on the streets. The bell over at the Dominicans reminded her that it was time to begin fixing her little supper, which she took every night alone in her salon. But hell, with the electricity off, how could she stew the prunes? Madame fumbled for her snuff can and carried it over to the window.

The Cine Olympia sign filled the heavens with an alternating murkiness of pink and black, pink and black.

11

CHARLIE CHAPLIN REVIVAL. The sign caught vermillion streaks on the prostitute's raincoat and made her eyes glow as she glanced from side to side at passers-by. She leaned against the wall near the ticket window of Cine Olympia. Her soliciting gaze dialogued with that of a fat middle-aged man until they recognized one another and both burst into laughter.

A long beam of dust-filled light poured from the projector onto the screen as the two walked down the aisle to their seats. Durand lighted a cigarette and then reached over and allowed his hand to rest on his companion's thigh.

"I don't think that's allowed in here," she whispered.

He moved his hand away.

"No, I mean the smoking, silly," she said and placed his hand where it had been. Durand's fingers kneaded the warm and fatty flesh through her cotton dress, and he thought how much it felt like the dough of his Irish wheat bread after its second rising.

"I'm sorry, M'sieu, but smoking is forbidden in the theater," the polite voice of an usherette said.

"Oh, a thousand pardons," he muttered and stamped the cigarette under his feet.

"I told you," the prostitute laughed.

"I knew it—but I always give it a try," he confided. "I get a few puffs that way at least. Say, what's that nice perfume you're wearing?"

"'Friendship's Illusion'," she said. "You'll have to get some for your wife—to remind you of me. Hm, I sure like you."

"Go on—I'm just a fat old man," he chided.

"That's what I like—somebody mature and experienced. Somebody you don't have to teach. Just sitting next to you excites me. Say, you're not really interested in this picture are you? Why don't we go where we can have some fun?"

"Hell, I've got to stay. A friend of ours is in the newsreel. My old woman'll quiz me about it when I get home. We've got plenty of time anyway," he added, putting his arm around her beefy shoulders.

Durand felt her hand come to rest heavily on his leg and he settled back to enjoy himself. There was no harm in profiting from the fondling while he watched the movie, and nothing was lost even if the tart did get suspicious after a while. It was a good turn. Slob—if she thought she'd get a sou of his money.

The movie house was a square box with much gold gilt. It smelled of cheapness and age and the dampness of people's clothes and shoes. Highlights from the screen were caught on the backs of empty seats. They relfected as crescents in Durand's glasses.

12

The red sanctuary lamp reflected on rows of empty pews as the monks knelt here and there reciting the rosary with some of the people of the quarter.

Father Gregoire hunched forward on his bulk, his attention distracted from the prayers by the doctor's remembered words. "You should have called me sooner. I've given him a hypo. He'll rest now. Bring him in tomorrow for x-rays. Yes, it's likely to be bad, I'm afraid."

Suddenly the powerful globe in the middle of the chapel flashed on with the returning electricity. It flooded the small room with light that annihilated the candles and struck Father Gregoire like a physical slap in the face. It blanched the walls to whiteness that throbbed against his eyes. He grimaced and shut out the onslaught by covering his face with his hands. The prayers droned on as though no one else had noticed. Squinting, Father Gregoire focused his attention away from the magnified lines of his palms and from their sweaty odor. But the tantalizing desire to go and wash them spread through his consciousness.

Hail Mary full of grace—"bring him tomorrow for x-rays." The smell of hands after a day of living—*The Lord is with thee*—"Yes, it's likely to be bad. . . ."

Father Gregoire lifted his head and glanced about. All the others, the monks, novices and people from the quarter stared into the spaces of their adoration, undisturbed in their prayers. Their faces and clothing had no dimensions under the bald light. Each looked as though he were cut from tin in an immovable attitude. White walls stared from their eyes and the tone of their murmurs was white.

A foot scraped against the floor, breaking the trauma. A head moved slightly to one side. Father Gregoire relaxed and as his eyes accustomed themselves to the sheet of light, dimensional perception returned with faint shadows and he saw the chapel as a hideous little box with much gold gilt which some of the older Fathers found beautiful.

He felt the sharp edge of the kneeling board through layers of callous on his knees. He felt it from the inside and was vaguely surprised to feel it from the inside.

He shook his head and closed his eyes and began again and tried to remember the prayers he had known from childhood.

13

Durand sat back in his seat and began laughing when an older model car with gas-burning headlamps rolled across the screen, the type of car he remembered seeing when he was a youngster.

It came to a steaming halt and a little man with baggy trousers climbed out, his moustached face radiating the comic poignancy of bewilderment.

Music from a warped record shrieked out to fill the theater as an accompaniment to the silent film.

14

"How can you stand it so loud," Aunt Louise scolded affectionately. She reached over and turned down the volume of Father Trissotin's radio until it was only a whisper, dampening, dear God, castrating the jubilant chorus of "Boys of the Old Brigade" that was being broadcast from the B.B.C.

Resentment pricked Father's nape but he contained himself and assumed the mask of benevolence which was his defense against his temper. He lowered the outer corner of his eyebrows and lifted the corners of his mouth while gazing sincerely at his powerful and heavily-veined hands.

"Bestow a blessing on those who persecute you," St. Paul had admonished in Sunday's Epistle—"a blessing, not a curse . . ." Dear God, it wasn't easy. He looked at his aunt's sparkling black eyes, so good and so lively, and felt that indeed it was impossible.

"Now if you want me to serve your supper in here, you'll have to clear some of this mess off of your desk," she chirped.

"All right, Auntie," he sighed. He glanced away toward the wall of books with their gold and silver titles aglitter in the lamplight. That "mess" as she called it—oh, not maliciously, but still with that saucy tone of hers—that "mess" was only the final version of his newest pamphlet into which he had, he could honestly say, put all his devotion to humanity and all his love for God and from which he prayed much good would come to the world. ". . . a blessing, not a curse . . ." Obediently he began to stack the pages at one side of his work table so that the nicely hand-lettered title faced up. Yes, there it was, for all Auntie gave a big damn, the fruit of much meditation and certainly one of his most succinct efforts: "Hints to Adolescents Who Do Not Wish to Appear Adolescent," ready to be printed and distributed to various churches and shrines all over the French-speaking world.

There had long been need for such a work to help the younger generation as was indicated by some of the more intelligent and sensitive lads who came to him for counsel.

"Here we are," Auntie Louise announced from the doorway. She carried the tray high and then deposited it on his desk with a flourish.

Father Trissotin closed his eyes for an instant to allow the intimate delight of sensing his antipathy for his aunt recede to its lowest and most forgiving ebb, as it did each night at this moment. As a creative cook she was unquestionably a genius, and Father was one to appreciate such gifts. He reached in his desk drawer for the special notebook to write down the recipes she had devised for this meal, recipes he intended someday to publish under the title: "The Parish Priest's Home Cook Book," as a help to other priests with refined palates whose housekeepers lacked the skills of his Auntie Louise.

"What have we tonight, Auntie?" he asked, bending to one side with his ears against the radio to catch a faint but splendid phrase of "Old Comrades" sung by the male chorus.

"Let me see," she mused while she lifted tops from the covered dishes and sniffed escaping vapors. "Ah, yes, you'll want the recipe for *Coquilles Saint-Jacques.*"

"That'll be fine Auntie. Ah, the food smells superb."

"Well, I'm sure it is," she said, then added her customary pietism. "I only mix the ingredients, God produces the goods."

Father brought a small portion of it to his mouth. His glance evolved slowly from one of interest to one of profoundest admiration.

The priest cherished the moments immediately following his evening "collation" as he called it. He referred to those moments as his quiet time. He turned down the lights until the shelves of books were little more than flecks of gold and silver from floor to ceiling in the tiny room that served as his study. Then, returning to his armchair, he slipped off his shoes, lifted his long and slender feet to the desk's edge and settled back to savor those leisurely processes of digestion that could evoke in him such an incomparable sense of well-being.

It was during this quiet time, Father observed privately, that the day's more tenaciously spiritual preoccupations underwent intimate transformation and became unashamedly animal preoccupations, as though the soul's proper habitation of the stomach could finally be given recognition over its more estimable habitation of places like the brain and heart. It must, he realized, be a secret delight—one of those unexplained mysteries that one enjoyed but did not discuss, for it was difficult to reconcile a certain refinement of tastes and cultures with the obvious truth that one's soul inhabited one's entire body, and was, in fact the form of the body itself. To an intelligent and sensitive man, even though this might be delicious to experience, it could still be repulsive to think of one's soul as inhering in, say, one's liver and gums and gall bladder; and certainly he was not alone in the world to be occasionally offended by this seeming lack of taste in God's design of humanity. But still, one obviously had to fight against such refined prejudgments. And when you had such food, such effortless digestion, such harmonious aftertastes on the palate, it was easy to believe, in private, that these unspiritual things were nevertheless among the choicest of God's gifts to his children.

But after all, wasn't there something spiritual about a really superlative meal like tonight's—spiritual in the sense of contact with a great art? Didn't its effects linger to enrich one's soul like those of any other superior emotion, giving one the same sense of uplift as an inspired performance of, say, Manon's "Gavotte"? Both great art and great cooking left man better spiritually than he was before experiencing them.

In any case, there was no need to torture himself with all these justifications. He would simply enjoy the aftermath of his dinner in the certainty—Desert Fathers to the contrary— that God smiled on his felicity. He reached over the sheaf of manuscript and turned up his radio. Music of the Coldstream Guards male chorus and band surged to full volume with a stirring performance of "The Empire is Marching". Father eased himself back in his chair and drifted into the heart of his private contentment under the spell of this glorious music.

15

Laughter was cut short by whitish flickers as the picture vanished from the screen and great inverted numerals flashed downward before the audience's eyes:

5

click

4

click

3

click

2

click

flap

flap

until new scenes appeared, jolting hearts that had been tuned to the past back to the present with the fanfare of NEWS OF THE WORLD, with a rooster's crowing above band music and athletes diving from high boards and soldiers marching and the sudden streak of an airliner across the screen that had only a moment before been host to an ancient touring car with gas-burning headlamps.

But all of this, too, clattered to a halt and became whitish flickers while the crowd moaned.

"Damned film breaks every week," Durand chuckled.

House lights flared and the spectators blinked at gold gilt interior.

"Are you about ready to go, Love?" the girl asked, shading her eyes with her hand.

"Where?" he asked innocently.

"Anywhere, Love, where we can get some friendship."

"How can we get more friendly than we've been?" he asked wide-eyed.

"Are you kidding me?" she snapped.

"We haven't settled on a price yet," he said.

"Five hundred francs, Love, and worth a lot more."

"Isn't that kind of small?" he pouted.

"What do you mean?"

"How about a thousand for a real good time?"

"Well, all right, Friend," she said smiling.

"In advance, naturally."

"Naturally."

"Have you that much with you?" he asked into her ear.

"What do you mean?" she bellowed, forgetting herself.

"Shhh. . ."

"Me pay you?"

"Why, I thought that was the idea all along," he said in a wounded voice. "You mean, you've been leading me on?"

"Why you dirty pig," she said loudly.

The audience's tittering outraged her. She floundered to her feet and pointed to Durand. "This man's a dirty pig. Leads a girl on," she screamed, mottling at their complacency. "That's what the pig did."

Durand hastily glanced around to ascertain that he knew no one among the audience. Then his features jelled into an expression of self-righteousness. He stared in front of him and declared it tit for tat. "She's the one that led me on. Temptress!"

"Sonofabitch!"

"I ask you," Durand said, spreading his hands out toward the blank screen and addressing his words to some invisible and higher judgment. "Who's to blame? I'm a decent married man, and a father too. But I'm only human. This, this—creature!—picks on such a man, takes advantage of his simple, naïve good nature. She arouses his baser instincts in the most calculated manner and then makes it even more sordid by demanding money."

"Why you . . ." the girl thundered. She stood before him with her hands on her hips, her face congested with fury. "You can't treat me like that! I'm no two-bit whore to be kicked around."

"Leave me alone," Durand commanded loudly in tones of profound injury. "I'll have none of the likes of you." He allowed his voice to tremble with indignation. "You ought to be ashamed. This is a family theatre, with decent people here." He tossed her raincoat to her. "Go peddle your wares elsewhere! Get out before I call the police."

"Who do you think you're talking to?" she shouted. "Why, I've slept with the nobility! I'm no cheap . . ."

"Shame," Durand said, and the word "shame" was chanted to her from all sides.

"Why, you, you bastards!" she cried above the chorus.

"Shame, shame, shame, shame," they sang pleasantly.

"Dirty pigs," she blathered, stumping up the aisle.

Durand glanced across the aisle to a fat, square-built woman whose stare was fixed on him in a glaze of revulsion. He nodded affably, winked and said: "I guess that's telling the bitch, eh, Madame?"

Madame Ponneger, there to begin her duties on behalf of her organization, gave him a violent snort of disgust.

In the immediate darkness with the repaired film focused on the screen, but with the sound track abandoned, Durand watched de Gaulle's dynamic facial expressions as he delivered a wordless speech. Durand leaned back in lonely splendor and told himself that it had indeed been a rich and full day. If only Flamart and Montausier could have been there to see the way he handled the whore.

16

Madame Culuhac, transfixed with horror, pressed her ear against the door and listened.

"Well, it's too bad," she heard Montausier say, his voice loud and hollow as it floated up the stairwell from the landing one story below.

"Leave me alone. Damn it!" the usually mild old Flamart shouted. "Just lay off me, sonofabitch!"

Hearing whores at prayer could not have dumbfounded Madame Culuhac more than hearing such belligerence from gentle Flamart. Why, it was unbelievable. Madame Culuhac cracked the door and looked out. In the dim light of the lower landing she saw Montausier with amused sympathy pat Flamart's shoulder. Then, bless her, if Flamart didn't lash out with his powerful arms and shove his friend hard against the wall.

"Leave me alone, I tell you!" he wailed before marching down the rest of the stairs.

Madame Culuhac closed the door and, leaning against it, stared blankly at the ornate little salon. She felt responsible for Flamart's frightening transition from the most docile of men into a giant of outrage, although, of course, it was not really her fault but that of those unprincipled bitches she had working for her.

The lights had been back on for over an hour now, and not one of the girls had returned to the house.

Madame felt despair rise in her bosom. Was this not another presage of the end? Wasn't there already talk tonight about a new *Société* out to clean up the quarter? Everyone knew what her massage emporium really was. Would she, a poor defenseless widow, stand a chance against the dirty blows the Christian women could so expertly deliver?

And what about her good name among the neighborhood men? Six customers had so far rung her bell, asking for treatments, only to be invited in for a gloomy drink and then turned away with whatever excuse she could muster, because there was simply no one there to give them their treatments. Ah, if these sluts could only have seen what it had done to dear Flamart to be sent away like that—unassuaged.

Well, she would tell the girls. That would make them feel
guilty, for all of them held him in rarest esteem. "Such a nice
old gentleman," they would say. "Such a relief from the regular run of Don Juans."

Yes, no one not in the business could appreciate what it
meant to have such an untroublesome and faithful client. And
since the death of old Ponneger last August there were few of
that quality left. He never, for instance, demanded some certain girl, like Montausier did—and then Montausier, that
smart bastard of a retired-lawyer-turned-philosopher would
always find some finical little detail not to his liking and back
down at the last moment, contenting himself merely with a
couple of glasses of cognac in the salon while he proceeded to
bore her to distraction with his brilliant intellectual observations. Did he really think it mattered so much as a big ding-
dong to her one way or the other whether the logical positivists
took metaphysics out of philosophy or left it in? Jesus.

Well, it was outrageous of the girls to stay away like that.
Simply outrageous. Madame Culuhac, having become one
flesh with Albert, rest him, and having remained that way for
twenty-six years, knew a thing or two about men; and certainly poor Flamart was the type to build himself up to something
and then—like all the quiet ones and the strong ones—to suffer far more than ordinary men when disappointed.

Noise rumbled up the hollow stairwell from a slammed
door downstairs. Madame Culuhac listened to the girls' footsteps and heard one loud cough. Hell, somebody would be laid
up soon enough.

17

"Come in, M'sieu . . ." the aged concierge smiled as she
opened the apartment-house door to Durand. "Come in. Ah,
what foul weather."

"Unforgivable of me to arouse you at this hour," Durand apologized.

"But not at all, M'sieu," she said, eyeing him devotedly from under her white lace nightcap. "Let me help you." She reached out and finished folding his dripping umbrella.

"Ah well, M'sieu—with so much on your mind, you know." The concierge raised one white eyebrow toward the upper landing in the direction of his apartment.

"Indeed," Durand sighed, remembering to allow his face muscles to sag into an expression that never failed to evoke concern from the old woman. He gazed at her and felt a certain expansion of pride. She was one of his hidden masterpieces.

On the surface of it, this was the hag face of all the concierges of Paris, the mean and sullen face with its touch of conniving sweetness, the withered little knot of a face with its habitual expression of disgust for humanity. But in Durand's presence, it was transformed by a delight entirely feminine and filled with undercurrents of pity and understanding. The other tenants could tip their hearts out and still she would blather when they forgot their keys and awakened her to open the door. Durand had seen in her the raw material for a project. He had taken the extra little trouble that changed her entire demeanor around him, and indeed probably her entire existence. For some time now, he had played the "wounded hero" in her presence, told her a few intimate and sincere lies about that pious wife of his, and had even intimated that on some cold and rainy night when Helene refused him her favors just once too often, he would be driven to barge into the concierge's quarters and give vent to all the pent-up passion she had inspired in him from that tragic day when he first saw her and realized that here was a woman with that rare and mature something he had desired. It was tragic because once a man perceived this mysterious quality, he was forever ensnared. Nothing but consummation could assuage his longing. And more tragic still because he could not, of course, tolerate the idea of being unfaithful to his wife no matter how unjustly she might treat him.

"Because she acts that way doesn't give me leave to abandon my own code, alas," he had informed his confidante one somber afternoon in the vestibule.

It had been the correct role to assume with her, Durand soon realized.

"M'sieu is pensive this evening," she whispered gently.

"No," he said with a wan smile. "Just tired, I suppose, discouraged . . . you know."

"Your mother-in-law is still there."

"Yes, alas," he said with a grimace.

"I don't see how you stand it, the way she treats you, M'sieu. She ought to thank God for a son-in-law."

"Well, she's elderly and religious—two guarantees of ill temper," Durand shrugged. He cast a stricken look at the concierge and turned slowly to mount the stairs.

With each step he felt an expression of consuming sweetness bore into his back, and he imagined her telling herself: "There goes that marvelous man whose life I've ruined. Will he never get over me?"

Did she really think he would someday burst into her little alcove room and confirm her best fears by seducing her? Probably not, Durand thought, but as long as he could charitably keep her uncertain about it, such a prospect would remain alive and wonderfully appalling for her to contemplate. He promised himself never to dishearten her with any cruel assurance of her safety at his hands or of his safety at hers. As it now stood, their relationship was so transparently beautiful to her, filling her life with that delicious remorse that could so bolster a person. And it was a pleasure for him as well to become, during those moments with her, a classic figure of tragedy wherein there was noble restraint as he went valiantly on with his life, trying to appear happy even though his body ached with love for her while remaining chaste in deference to a higher principle of morality that the rest of the world certainly did not suspect him of owning. That was their shared intimacy. She alone knew the real Durand. To the rest, his bawdy reputation was only a gallant cover-up.

"Good night, M'sieu," her voice sifted up the narrow stairwell.

"Good night," he answered softly, adding "dear friend."

It was an excellent touch, he told himself, to increase the term of endearment each time in order to give the relationship an illusion of growth. The last time, about three weeks ago, it had been "dear, dear Madame" and tonight it was "dear friend" and he could proceed from there on through the dearests, the darlings and on and on. It reflected back on a man with the pleasure of giving, but it might be wise to mark these progressive endearments down somewhere so he could recall expressions at any literate man's fingertips to keep this old girl going far beyond her life-expectancy span, but still that was no excuse to be profligate of them, or to risk losing one's place. One did not, for example, go from "my adored one" slipshod back to "my darling" without taking on one's shoulders the responsibility of causing tormenting doubts. He would most certainly keep them jotted down somewhere. But where? On the baseboard of the second-floor water closet? No, she would be sure to see them and guess when she cleaned the little room. But where? It had to be just the right place.

He stopped on the darkened landing outside his apartment. Bal-musette music with its bright accordions drifted faintly from the third floor, like the sounds of a distant carnival. Its cheapness fitted the night, the old building. Durand hesitated at his door. Above the muffled strains, he heard the drone of his wife's and mother-in-law's conversation. The vague mushroom odor of dampness, of old rooms and unaired carpets rose around him. He put off the moment of entering his apartment and concentrated on squeezing the final portion of pleasure from his meditation. Where would he mark his endearments? It had to be a truly fitting.

On the thigh of that statue in the Breville Museum down

the street? Of course. He was, after all, an artist in his own private way, he told himself. With his quietly adventurous sense of the livingness of things he made a splendid time of it for himself. And this inspiration was just another proof of it. Others like old Flamart lived out the dull routine of their lives, but he made something exciting of his. The statue was a really luminous idea. Durand heard the music flourish to a halt and an announcer's voice rise enthusiastically above scattered applause. He started down the stairwell to the floor of black and white tiles far below in the vestibule and chuckled to himself. That dumb-looking statue sprawled on her back. The way she supported herself on her elbows, buttocks and heels, as though she could scarcely bear the coldness of the marble slab beneath her, with her knees slightly flexed and spread apart in an attitude of shameless exposure, had caused a good deal of debate among the neighborhood men. He, for example, had never been able to decide whether she was waiting for her lover or her gynecologist. Montausier contended that she was sun-bathing under the radiance of an Athenian sky with perfect godlike naturalness and nothing more. On the other hand, Flamart was always discountenanced in the way that masculine men can be embarrassed, not by naked women but by nude art. Durand's reaction was somewhere between Montausier's reverent appreciation of *The Reclining Diana* and Flamart's blushing distaste—she was simply a big howl to cheer him on dark days. He could never look at that stoic expression on her face without an upsurge of gleeful sympathy in recollection of Flamart's crude remark that on a cold day it must be as bad for her as "sitting bare-assed on the frozen Seine."

Yes, that was the perfect solution. He would mark his progressive endearments on her classic thigh alongside all the little obscenities scrawled there by neighborhood youngsters. Lord, it was broad enough to contain the text of at least half of *Le Petite Larousse* if one didn't write too large.

Edith Piaf's voice cut through the hall emptiness from

the radio upstairs. With a final glance down through the silhouette of stair-railing to the checkerboard parquet below, so cold and deserted at this hour, Durand opened the door to his apartment. The voices of his wife and mother-in-law lashed down the hall with strident liveliness of pistons in perpetual motion. He listened while he slipped out of his heavy overcoat, telling himself that if he heard just one mention of "Our Dear Lord and Savior" he would go back outside and sit on the stairs until Helene's mother left. No, it was safe, they were discussing a friend's uterus.

He shut the door loudly, heard their conversation falter and then resume with all its vigor. He ambled across the entrance hall to the kitchen where he saw a jar of strawberry preserves and a dish of butter on the dented tin drainboard. Couldn't they put anything away? And why didn't they give him some sort of greeting? They'd heard him come in, but because belle-mere would start vibrating if her daughter left her to go kiss the tired husband. Well, that's the way it was, he told himself. She'd never say anything, of course, but there'd be that brooding sort of sourness over the house for hours afterward. From almost directly overhead he heard Piaf's tortured voice sing: "Tell me I'm your dove / the only one that you love." Well, he was hungry. He would prepare something to eat, but first he would let them see that he, at least, had the basic good manners to greet them.

"Hello, anybody home?" he called through the kitchen door toward the living room in his most jovial voice.

"Hello!" they answered with exaggerated cheeriness.

"Have a nice day?" he called to Helene.

"Fine, Honey, did you?"

"Fine."

You all right, Mama?"

"Fine," she said and then lowered her voice in renewed conversation with Helene.

"My joy in being home," he announced to the kitchen walls, "is truly boundless." Ah, well, never mind, he told him-

self as he walked over and stood on tiptoe to urinate into the
metal sink. He listened, gazing blankly at the stained plaster
wall above the sink.

"Hell. . ." he groaned softly. He turned on the faucet full
force and stepped away from the splash with his middle while
he bent forward to wash his hands. Piaf's voice was lost in the
rumble.

Well, now for some food. He would fix the women a little
something too. The butter had not been touched. There were
no dirty dishes. Perhaps they'd been waiting for his return to
have a snack. They would enjoy his bread—nothing so good
on a cold night as warm home-made bread, prepared from the
Irish wheat recipe he so prized, and baked into fragrant loaves
that made the old apartment smell like a wheat field in August.

He finished wiping his hands on his handkerchief and got
out one of the large dark loaves that were wrapped in thin towels. He felt his paunch sag against his belt when he leaned forward to slice the bread. At least two slices each—that would
make six.

Now, to put his bread into the oven to warm it through
without toasting it too hard. It had to be just right. Oh, yes, by
God, he has his own private world of artistry, some things he
could really do well, and bread was part of that world. But like
all creative accomplishments it was nerve-wracking and
Durand grew as fidgety over his bread as a pianist over a con-
certo.

He uncapped the preserves and felt the kitchen lonely,
Lord, lonely. Then he put on water for the tea. The women
had never tasted this particular mixture of jasmine which
Julien had brought back from Indo-China. Ah, dear lad, if he
were there, he'd be in the kitchen helping his old man. But
he'd been right, of course, to go chasing off to Dijon after that
girl of his.

Durand cracked the oven door and sniffed outpuffings of
yeasty sweetness with the passionate gratification of the artist.
It was exactly, precisely, to-the-point right. He left the oven

door open, hoping the women would smell it and make some mention of the aroma. Their conversation rambled on and new waves of loneliness filled the kitchen. When he pried the top from the canister of tea, a fresh clean fragrance of flowers detached itself. He scratched through his thinning hair. They would love to smell the tea. He would take it in and stick it under their noses so they could sniff the jasmine blossoms.

". . .and she hardly has any hair," Helene said when he walked through the door. "And she's—let's see . . ."

"Four months old," Mama put in primly. "She looks like a Mongol to me, but you could never come right out and . . ."

"Here," Durand interrupted. He smiled pleasantly and held the canister under his mother-in-law's nose which flared delicately and turned white on the tip whenever he entered their presence. "Take a whiff of that, eh? How . . ."

"Mmm, yes," she said absently. "Exquisite."

"Darling," he said and offered the canister to his wife's nose. She inhaled and raised her eyebrows in appreciation.

". . . and would you believe it," Mama resumed to Helene, "she's already feeding that child meats."

Durand lifted the can to his nose and limped over the worn carpet back to the kitchen. He limped with melancholy as he had done since childhood whenever anything dispirited him.

In moments like this he took refuge in the strong words of other men, and a phrase from Bloy, over which he and Montausier had enjoyed much laughter, came to mind: "A woman saint may fall into the mire and a prostitute may ascend to the light, but never will either of them be able to become a respectable woman, because the appallingly barren cow known as the respectable woman is eternally powerless to escape from her nothingness either by falling low or mounting high."

Remembering such words was enough for Durand, who felt the same sense of release the author must have felt in writing them.

The odor at the door shocked him from his reverie. He hurried across the room, grabbed crocheted pot holders and lifted the pan of bread from its rack. As he placed squares of sweet-cream butter on the coarse brown pores, pride assuaged him. This would be one of those triumphs of simple fare; nothing but the bread with its butter and strawberry preserves, and cups of hot jasmine tea—a connoisseur's fare of rarest perfection. And it was universal. No one, no matter how untutored or how super-refined his palate, could fail to be enchanted by it.

He placed it on a tray. It was ready. He bent forward and inhaled. All was freshness and health. The strawberries smelled of shaded fruit on a summer's day. It was the French countryside brought into the midst of a wintry Paris night.

You're just worn out, aren't you?" he heard Mama say to Helene as he stepped into the living room.

Of course she was, he thought in self-reproach, with all of her work and worry about the boy being gone. That's why she hadn't come into the kitchen to help him. He could, for a moment, honestly detest Bloy for what he'd said about women like Helene and her mother. The tea and fresh bread would restore her, and she would feel fine by bedtime. You had to understand these things.

He set the tray on the marble mantelpiece and stood to pour the tea.

"What do you take in your . . ."

"Lemon and sugar, please," Mama said.

"A touch of milk in mine," Helene said.

It sounded like a damned cafe, he thought with new resentment, but realized he was being touchy. They couldn't know of his nervousness, his need for applause as he brought out his masterpiece for their approval. He poured their cups and jasmine-scented steam hazed his glasses. Despite the cold, he felt sweat moisten his underclothes. He measured sugar and lemon into one cup, milk into another, but nothing in his, of course.

Turning to them he plastered a smile all over his face, because there was love—passion even—and it was stupid to feel hurt because no one kissed him or offered to help in the kitchen; and also because there needed to be a cheerful atmosphere, freed of all constraint, if his bread were to carry its most pleasurable effect.

He beamed encouragingly and bent down with the tray.

"Well," Mama said, staring at Helene. "Just what *did* Father Trissotin say about going to the movies?" She served herself from the tray.

"He said there was nothing wrong with going to the movies, but that we should abstain from it during Lent because it doesn't look well, it scandalizes non-Catholics, and it . . ."

"Well, what about freedom of the will, for God's sake?"

"I don't know. I'm just telling you what he said at Mass. No movies during Lent. He wants all of us to get closer to God," Helene explained. She took her tea and bread on the arm of her chair and glanced appreciatively toward her husband.

Durand deposited the tray on the coffee table and was serving himself from it when he saw Mama jerk her skirt back to the upper part of her thigh, to avoid spilling anything on it, and balance her snack on her bony knees. It was a common mannerism of hers, but the sight of her bared flank never failed to offend Durand. It caused him to be thankful that he did not share in their faith, for it was his understanding that after the final judgment in paradise, the souls of the faithful would rejoin their bodies and all would walk about innocently naked; and it was simply more that he could stomach to imagine running into Mama under such conditions.

"Well, did you know that "The Unfortunate One," with Edwige Desplaches and Pierre Martucci, opens at the Cine Olympia the first Friday in Lent?"

"Oh no . . ." Helene moaned.

"And I've been counting on us going. What are you limping about, Charles?" asked Mama.

"Nothing."

"You're too fleshy. You ought to take some of that off. Weight compresses the discs, you know."

Durand carried his plate to the couch and was lifting the cup to his mouth when he saw Mama tear off the exquisite crust of his bread and lay it to one side while she nibbled at the soft inner portion. He closed his eyes against the desecration and then opened them, waiting for some reaction to illuminate her face. At any moment Durand expected her to stop in the middle of her munching, turn toward him with her eyes widening in astonishment and say: "My God, Charles, did you make this magnificent bread?"

She swallowed, sipped quickly at her tea and exclaimed: "Well, I can't see any sin in us going to see such a spiritual picture as 'The Unfortunate One'. It's all about this beautiful girl who prefers to be torn to pieces by animals rather than allow herself to be deflowered by the brute of a caravan leader."

"I know," Helene said sadly. "But Father Trissotin says Lent is a time of sacrifice. We have to obey."

"What do you think about it, Charles?" Mama asked, glaring at Durand.

"About what?" he sighed, lowering his untouched cup back into his plate.

"About having to obey Father Trissotin."

"You do, I guess, if you accept him as your spiritual director."

"Well, what about freedom of the will, for God's sake?"

"I don't know anything about it. I guess it means you're free not to obey, free to go to hell so far as that's concerned," he observed wearily, without realizing the double significance of his last phrase and then mightily pleased by it.

"Do you mean to tell me it's a sin to go to a movie—especially such a spiritual one as that?" She tore off a bite of bread and chewed rapidly.

"No, mother," Helene put in. "But it's a sin to disobey."

Durand closed his eyes against the sight of her bolting the bread he had stayed up until midnight the preceding night baking so they might have a special treat. He clamped his mouth shut against shouting, "What about my goddamn bread?" and instead he interrupted casually with: "Do you like this kind of bread?"

Mama stopped her tirade and looked at the chunk she held between her fingers, as though she were only then aware of it.

"Yes, it's good" she said. "Is there any more tea?"

"Yes, plenty," he said, feeling bitter kinship with all those artists whose masterpieces were unappreciated by their swinish contemporaries. At least she liked the tea. "It's awfully good, this is jasmine, isn't it?"

"Mm . . . yes. It's very nice."

"I'll have some too, while you're up dear," Helene said with an encouraging smile.

Wondering what had so crippled them that they were incapable of serving themselves, Durand carried their cups back to the kitchen. This was like asking a Cortot or Menuhin to distribute programmes at their concerts. Acids formed a knot of resentment in his throat, but above all the immediate private growlings and grumblings, the saintly harmonies of jasmine and wheat bread consented to intertwine themselves the instant he stepped into the kitchen.

"Dear?" he heard Helene call him.

"Yes?"

"You need to put about one and a half spoons of tea to the cup when it's as . . ."

"I know how to make tea," he flared, and heard a "Humph" full of partisan significance from Mama. This was the first goddamn jasmine tea they'd ever seen, smelled or tasted, but they had to hand out their instructions. And you could have served them strawberries on sawdust for all they noticed.

"Just when is Easter this year?" he heard Mama ask.

"I don't know," Helene said. "I'll have to look it up." Interest livened her voice.

Her tone encouraged Durand and he poured the tea with hope in all the smells, hope in the roof and walls of their home, telling himself again that all you needed was patience and the gift of silence.

He nudged up his glasses, rubbed his tired eyes with his forefingers and swallowed the knot. Then he set the smile on his face and returned to the living room with fresh cups of tea.

"Do you mind," Mama asked him as soon as he appeared, if Helene and I see the movie anyway?"

"No, I don't mind."

"Well, if he's sure he doesn't mind spending the evening alone?" Helene said.

Durand smiled down at her and was about to expand himself with a generous remark.

"After all," Mama cut in. "He's gone every day while you're stuck here all the time."

Durand felt the smile become fixed and hurriedly brought his tea to his lips.

"If I thought it was a sin, of course, I'd never think of going. But I don't think the Lord ever meant for Lent to be made ridiculous. Do you Charles?"

"Do you?" she asked again.

"I don't know anything about it," he said.

"I can't see anything sinful about it. Especially when you think of what some people do and then show up with children that look like Mongols, why, my God, it's . . ."

"Mother," Helene reproached.

"Well, it's certainly—evident—let's say, that there's a snooker in there somewhere. Priests attack us for going to the movies but they never seem to wonder about someone like . . ."

A blasphemous vision settled before Durand's eyes, a truly frightening tableau of Mama being nailed on a cross by a ignorant parish priest while in the distance a red neon sign flickered off and on "The Unfortunate One" in the storm-wracked skies above the Golgotha Cine Olympia.

"What are you grinning about?" Mama broke in.

"Nothing."

"Yes you were, now Charles. What was it?"

He saw Helene's smile of sympathy for him, saw tenderness soften her eyes. Warmth for her flooded through his tired belly.

"Oh, I was just thinking about something a fellow told me at the shop today," he said evasively.

"Well, what was it?" Mama's voice intruded into the silent exchange between Helene and him.

He was tempted to tell her the truth, to describe his vision of her crucifixion, but passed it off with: "Well, it's kind of a dirty little story, but awfully fun . . ."

"Then please don't tell it," she said stonily. "You know perfectly well, if there's anything I can't bear, it's smut."

Even Helene frowned. Durand stirred from his seat, feeling new affection for Bloy. "I'll clean up in the kitchen," he sighed.

"I'll get it, dear," Helene said, not moving from her chair.

"No—you two go ahead and have a nice visit."

In the kitchen he took one long look at the mess, placed the tray on the sink and went to his room to get ready for bed.

He was undressing when he heard Mama's voice through the thin door.

"What's he so grumpy about tonight?"

"Why, he's not grumpy."

"Yes he is. I can always tell."

"Well, he's had a long day, poor darling. His back is bothering him, too."

Durand slipped the outsized cotton nightgown over his head.

"Where's he gone?"

"Probably to bed."

"I thought he was going to clean up the kitchen for you."

"I'll get it in the morning."

"Well, he might have mentioned something about being glad I came over."

Durand listened. Mama was sounding like a concierge again. God's love, she was there every day in addition to her one evening a week. Did she expect him to say he was glad every time?

What if he should do the very thing she always prided herself on doing—be frank, tell the absolute truth. "I always find it's best in the long run," she would say as a prelude to the slaughter. Yes, what if he should step in and say that he was not glad she came?

Durand fished the gown loose from his pauch, felt it descend over his body and brush at his ankles.

She really didn't know why he was grumpy? Lord, how could she help knowing? But they probably had all sorts of secret longings and justifications that he knew nothing about.

He opened the living room door and stepped two paces forward on his bare feet,

"I think I'll go to bed now. A long day. You two have a nice visit. Certainly nice having you, Mama," he said in a voice devoid of any pretense of sincerity.

"I enjoyed it, Charles," she answered in the same tone.

In their bedroom, Durand plopped down in a chair, lifted his feet to the edge of the bed and switched on the radio. Walls of cheap flowered paper—giant red poppies on a black lattice-work design, pulsed against his tired eyes. It was Helene's room really, for there was nothing of him in it except his clothes thrown over a chair in the corner. The church calendar on the wall near the window, opened to January, with a painting of "Christ in the Temple" was hers. The Sacred Heart statue on the little bracket shelf over their night table was hers. The many charcoal and pastel drawings of the saints that she rather skillfully executed were hers. The pile of religious pamphlets on the radio table was hers. He noticed that she had once again left a little blue one by Father Trissotin, entitled

Marriage on top of the stack. It could be intriguing, a book on marriage, but he was not going to pick it up as she obviously hoped he would. All of it was hers, all of it was religious. Lord. But if it made her happy. . . .

Above the radio's warming hum, organ music boomed forth, distant and full of echoes as though broadcast from some vast cathedral. He leaned forward with his elbows on his knees, his ear close to the speaker, and listened to the chromatic introspection of a chorale. From that vantage he saw a patch of white under the bed. Reaching down, he pulled forth a large poster, hand-lettered by Helene.

He propped it against the wall and resumed his chair to admire it. It was certainly one of the finest jobs Helene had done in his series of "Quotes from Great Books" that he hung about his store as a merchandising method, primarily, and also because such things delghted him and edified his customers. Montausier had found this quote and Helene had block-printed the poster in huge letters. It was so good he would put it in his store window for a few days and perhaps build a display of art books around it. A really capital idea. Nudging his glasses up to the bridge of his nose, Durand squinted and read carefully the quote from Jacques Maritain's *Creative Intuition in Art and Poetry*: "Let us look at human faces as if they were pictures, then the pleasures of our eyes will be multiplied. An Epicurean of art traveling in New York subways enjoys a ceaselessly renewed exhibition of Cezanne's, Hogarth's or Gauguin's pictures offered free of charge by nature, or of Seurat's when all the lights are on."

She had glued color postcard reproductions of works by Cezanne, Hogarth, Gauguin and Seuarat to each of the four corners, since few in the quarter were apt to know these artists as intimately as a person like Durand, who for years had examined each new art book that came into his store. It was only after reading Maritain's statement that Durand realized how much, in his pleasant search for nude and seductive poses, he had absorbed about art. He decided to surround the poster with a display of illustrated booklets on Cezanne, Utrillo, Gauguin, Chagal, Degas, Matisse and so forth, and also some of the expensive new Skira editions.

Durand removed his glasses and relaxed with his head back against the chair headrest, absently listening to the organ recital. He closed his eyes and sought to project faces as paintings against his eyelids, as Maritain advised.

Helene? She was many: a matronly Vermeer preparing Sunday dinner in the kitchen, or a thick-bodied and rosy Reubens, sitting there naked on the straight-backed chair serenely drawing on her dark hose every morning.

And Montausier? Yes, a fine-lined and stern-faced l'Armessin engraving of some seventeenth-century nobleman.

And old Flamart? Yes, a placid Vlaminck winter scene.

That whore tonight? She was a broad-hipped Maillol nude lying on her stomach across a couch, reading a letter.

Madame Carnot at the tobacco shop? She was a Chardin, an old lady cleaning fish or something.

Splendid images passed slowly behind Durand's closed eyelids.

And who else?

Mademoiselle Mailleferre? Yes, she was a Rouault, or rather the way it might look were Rouault to paint a portrait of Baudelaire.

And Mama? She was a Goya etching from the "Horrors of War" series.

Himself? He was many in different moods: a Hals "Cavalier" minus moustache one moment; a "Country Squire" by Bonnard; and the top figure in Rodin's "The Kiss" dissolving consciousness in passion . . .

"Darling?"

Durand opened his eyes to a bleared view of his wife among giant red poppies and the sound of hot jazz from the radio.

"You'd better get to bed, hadn't you?" she suggested.

He roused himself with a grunt and flicked off the radio.

"Darling, are you all right?" she asked. Durand quickly looked up at her. "Mother's still here, but I had to see you for a moment," she said. "There's something wrong, isn't there? I can sense it. I've felt it all evening." Her eyes opened in concentration on his face, peered into it with an intensity secret to her.

Durand pulled her easily into his lap.

"No, there's nothing wrong now," he whispered against her ear, wondering how anyone no larger than she could weigh so heavily.

"Are you sure?"

"Yes, everything's fine."

He felt her relax in his arms and allow herself to respond to his caresses.

"Your bread was just perfect tonight," she said.

"Did you like it?" Durand murmured against her throat, while his fingers unbuttoned her blouse. He felt her hand under his chin as she guided his face upward and placed her mouth over his.

"It was delicious—the best you've ever baked," she whispered against his cheek when the long kiss was over. "Honey, I was over at the Dominicans for Vespers this evening. I told Father Gregoire what an expert baker you are. . ."

"I'm sure he's not interested in this kind of baking," Durand said.

"I thought it might be nice if you'd take some bread to them once in a while."

Durand lifted his face away and frowned at her.

"Don't be suspicious," she cajoled. "I'm not trying to get you inside the place. I'll even take it myself. The novices need the nourishment and that bread's almost a meal in itself the way you fix it. There's one boy in particular. He's sick. Father Gregoire says he needs better food. I just thought if our Julien were in such a place . . ."

"God forbid."

". . . how much we'd appreciate it if someone did a thing

like this." Her mouth closed over his again, and Durand wondered if she meant they'd appreciate it if someone gave Julien this kiss or the wheat bread. The intimacy aroused jubilance in his body. A glow of pride spread warmly over every inch of his flesh beneath the nightgown.

Rain poured against the closed shutters. Durand felt the closed-in deliciousness of the room, aware of their long experience of enthusiasm for her body which was as thoroughly his as for his own.

"Such young things we do," she murmured appreciatively. "I'll come back as soon as she leaves."

"All right. . ."

Durand helped her disengage herself and get to her feet. He watched her button her blouse and touch her hair into place. The sight of her transforming herself back into the respectable guise of a middle-aged woman delighted him, as it delighted him to share glances of sympathy with her while she waited a moment to allow herself to cool from pinkness to whitness.

He thought it strange that she should tiptoe out of the room when she left to rejoin her mother, the way one would tiptoe from a library or church or some other hallowed place.

Lounging back in his chair, he basked in anticipation of her return. He squinted down the length of his body and saw the whiteness of his gown somewhat like the whiteness of those Dominican robes, and he envisioned himself with his hair cut in that funny Dominican tonsure, dressed in white robes with a denim apron. He stood before the ovens of some medieval monsatery kitchen, and in all the cells, all the corridors, monks inhaled the aroma of his Irish wheat bread and thanked God for old Friar Charles.

So the Dominicans would like some of his bread? The idea pleased him. Mama could scorn it, but he'd wager those young novices would know how to appreciate it. And what would Montausier say? It would be worth it just to see the expression on his face.

"Yes, you'll have to excuse me. I have to get home early

so I can bake the Domincan's bread." It was a nice touch, tossed off nonchalantly like that, and would certainly give Montausier the colic.

Too, the thought of providing bread that would nourish the bone and sinew and muscle and organs of the young novices, men who might someday become holy, seemed a particularly gallant gesture toward their God, coming from a person who did not believe in Him. Durand felt the magnanimity of it dilate his finest instincts as a gentleman.

Squinting again, he saw his Dominican robe become a white cotton nightgown, smelling of soap and bulging with the contours of his body. He glanced at his bare feet with their short, stubby toes and neatly cropped toenails.

Through the door, he heard the women begin their goodnights. It would take them an hour to finish, he thought. Switching off the lamp, he crawled in between the sheets of his bed and rolled to the far side. He pulled the gown up to his chest, drew the sheet over him and allowed the palm of his hand to rest affectionately on the bare flesh of his belly.

"Oh, listen, Precious, there was one more thing I wanted to tell you," he heard Mama say.

"Really? What was that?" Helene asked without enthusiasm.

Mama's voice dropped to an almost inaudible tone, the way it did when she shared confidences.

Durand watched the slit of light under the door for a while and then closed his eyes against the room's darkness.

18

Father Gregoire winced at the loud rustle of his straw mattress as he turned over in his cot. He was drifting back to the heart of sleep when he heard the cry again, thin and muffled as though it were part of a memory or a dream.

He struggled for wakefulness. Distantly he heard dripping like a water faucet or rain from the eaves and his eyes gradually focussed on the yellowish square where reflected light from the streetlamps below came through his window onto the ceiling.

A high scream shattered the monastic silence.

The cold plank floor beneath his bare feet shocked the monk to full wakefulness and to the double awareness that his years of monastic training had made habitual—awareness of the immediate scene where someone cried out in the dark, and simultaneous awareness of God's invisible presence.

With trembling muscles he threw his white robes over his pajamas. Isolated fragments of a song floated through the silent building and Father guessed that Friar Lupe must be out of his head from the hypodermic he had received. The monk slipped his feet into sweat-dampened shoes and hurried out into the hall without waiting to tie the laces.

Two cell doors clicked shut when he turned on the light. Others were hearing then . . .

Father's shoes rumbled on the wooden floors and the metal tips of his laces clacked in magnified loudness over the Great Silence.

Passing closed doors, he felt the dense and tangible wakefulness of monks and novices lying in their cells, staring into darkness and muttering prayers for their tormented brother.

Lupe's brown form was spotlighted in the widening beam from the hall light when Gregoire opened the door. The boy lay on his side, curled up in a ball with his hands clasped between his thighs. His blankets lay in a pile at the foot of his cot. On the wall above the bed, gazing serenely down on the friar's back, Father noticed the shadowed crucifix.

The monk stepped into the room and bent to look into Lupe's face. Open eyes glistened unseeing in an expression of concentration, as though the boy were intent upon remembering something deep within himself. His mouth hung slack, and though the room was frigidly cold, his teeth did not chatter. He hummed to himself, a wierdly sweet melody, more terrible than the screams had been.

"Lupe . . . Lupe," the monk whispered, shaking the boy's sinewy shoulder. His touch unlocked a reaction of uncontrolled trembling. He lifted the friar easily to the center of the cot and spread the blankets over him. He stepped away to go telephone the doctor when a paroxysm jerked Lupe up to a wobbly sitting position. The priest hurriedly seated himself on the side of the cot with his arm around the boy. His free left hand raked across the table top in search of the glass. It was no longer there. Congestion mounted in the friar's body. Father felt behind him, flicked open the bed-table door and his fingers closed around the handle of the chamber pot. It sloshed, detaching an odor of cold urine. Depositing it on the floor, he quickly placed his hand under Lupe's mouth to catch the outpouring phlegm.

A shadow fell across the boy's face and Father glanced up to see the tall silhouette of Marie-Martin in the doorway.

"He's out of his head from the dope," Father Gregoire said. "And he's freezing. Will you fix him some hot tea and bring a charcoal brazier in here?"

Marie-Martin bowed and turned to go.

"Father?" Gregoire said.

The tall figure hesitated.

"First would you hand me a towel?" Lupe's sigh rasped loud in the room. Holding his soiled left hand away, Father Gregoire lowered the boy back onto his pillow. He felt Marie-Martin cleansing his hand with a towel. Then the other monk's footsteps passed out the door and down the corridor. "Who's there?" Friar Lupe asked.

"It's Father Gregoire, Lupe . . ."

"Is it late?"

"Yes."

"Is it already the Great Silence?"

"Yes."

"I talked without permission," Lupe said desolately.

"That's all right, Lupe. Do you hurt?"

"Yes. . .all over. Where are my pajamas?"

"You've been too sick for us to put them on you."

The monk listened to the boy's struggles to speak past some impediment in his throat.

"Father." he gasped. "I'm just praying I don't vomit."

"We're fixing you some hot tea. It'll settle your stomach."

"If I vomit, I'll just . . ."

"Try to think of something else."

Gregoire picked up the chamber pot and rose to go empty it in the event Lupe should become nauseated again.

"So I just told this old woman at the gate. . . . Did I already tell you about her?" the friar asked suddenly. He raised his head and stared into the hall light. "Where are you?" he asked, his voice rising in panic.

"Here I am . . . standing right beside you."

"Oh . . . did I tell you about the old woman?"

"No. But why don't we wait and talk about it tomorrow?"

"It was so funny. I thought I'd already told you," Lupe laughed. His head dropped back to the pillow. "Father?"

"Yes, Lupe."

"Are you really my father?" the boy asked distantly, slipping into the familiar form of address which children use with their parents.

"I'm one of your fathers, Lupe."

"It wouldn't be too terrible then if I did have to vomit in front of you, would it?" he asked as though the question were gravely important to him.

"It wouldn't be terrible at all . . ."

"Father?" Lupe said, his voice rising high and bodiless in delirium.

New tremblings shook the cot. Gregoire looked down on Friar Lupe's agitated face behind which the invisible struggle mounted to climax.

"Don't leave me. I'm afraid," he gasped abjectly as though the confession were wrenched from him against his will.

The monk reached forward and lifted the boy to a sitting postion. He cradled Lupe's head against his chest and pulled the blankets around to keep the friar's back warm.

"Is Mama cooking supper?" Lupe asked, his voice muffled against the fold of the prior's robe.

Gregoire answered by patting Lupe's head. He felt the short bristles of tonsured hair against his palm. In the silence, stairs creaked with Father Marie-Martin's returning footsteps. Gregoire held the bundled boy closer, noting that the rigours came in decreasing waves.

The beam of light widened when the other monk shouldered the door open and entered carrying a bowl of tea in one hand and the charcoal brazier in the other. He placed the tea on Lupe's bed table and adjusted the brazier on the floor beside the cot.

"It'll heat better if we close the door," he suggested.

"Yes, please. And turn on the light."

The bulb flickered to full brightness, bringing into focus the scrubbed floor planking, old and mealy, and the sweating walls; it gave the cell its diminsions of extreme narrowness.

"Shall I help you give him the tea?" Marie-Martin asked.

"Let's let him rest a moment."

"Is his mind still wandering?"

"Yes, he thinks he's at home and I'm his father. You'd better call the doctor again."

Marie-Martin bowed with the natural and simple movement of a true monk, half-bending forward with his hands clasped together beneath his scapular. His glance fell on the chamber pot and he took it with him when he left.

Gregoire waited, sitting in a position that grew increasingly uncomfortable, with his heavy trunk twisted around the head of the cot. He glanced idly about the cell. On the floor, near his unlaced shoe, he saw Lupe's rosary where the boy had apparently dropped it in his delirium. He stretched down to retrieve it, brought it to his lips and then placed it on the table beside a tattered little volume of prayers. The cell, in this raw light, was all poverty. How little there was of Lupe in it, Father thought: a cheap red toothbrush at the back of his table. The rest belonged to the community—the crucifix on the wall, the white robes, mud-splattered at the the hem, which someone had neatly folded over the straight-back chair, even the heavy black shoes under the cot. And yet it was permeated with Lupe as one of many who passed through it, leaving no other trace than the invisible one of prayer, desiring to leave no other trace—a room where a soul loved, where that alone was happiness, that alone important.

A flushing toilet whitened the silence. A moment later Marie-Martin opened the cell door and placed the chamber pot near the cot before going to telephone the doctor.

Through his palm on the boy's head, Father Gregoire felt a steady heartbeat. He waited, holding the friar quietly and watching the youthful head relax forward on tendons until he looked down on a slim, unwrinkled neck, hard against the whiteness of his robe.

Currents of warmer air radiated from the brazier. Father felt faint heat against the flesh above his shoetop. He moved to ease the sleeping friar back into a reclining position.

"No. . ." the word was groaned, a frail plea that halted the monk.

Lightning altered the inside light and turned the room white with phosphorescence. Rain returned, splattering in gusts against the glass. Gregoire looked up to see the window transformed into a mirror. It reflected back the image of a thick-featured and gross person, distinguished from the least distinguished of men only by his white robes and silvering tonsure. The man sat on a cot and held a blanket-covered youth in his arms. Father Gregoire's back ached from the unnatural position. He looked at the image in the window again and saw himself as all fathers out there in the night, awakened from slumber to hold their troubled children in the security of embrace, to absorb in their older and thicker bodies the fevers and fears of the younger ones; men who could look down on the troubled flesh of their children and for a time know the unfathomable perfectibility of love—and be lifted high, high within themselves.

Drowsily he heard the slow tolling of midnight from the great bell of the clock tower over the *Palais de Justice*. The cold, the emptiness, the poverty, the sickness—all of it gathered into a momentary pattern of harmony, stemming from some mysterious concordance wherein the Divine intermingled with this slumbering body and touched with holiness the least folds of its flesh and the meanest of its functions; with love as the keynote of all the interminglings of heaven and earth; love as the bridge that joined the two.

He listened, resting in its warmth until the bells died finally away to silence, and he could hear nothing but the rain that fell steadily over the rooftops of the quarter.

19

From the deep comfort of her feather bed, Madame Ponneger saw the enormous rain drops pelt against her window and heard the same clangor of bells echo away into quietness.

Closing her eyes, she prayed silently for success in the *Société*'s campaign to rid the quarter of smut. At the end, her large voice boomed out in the unearthly hush of her room.

"Amen."

PART TWO

THE SECOND TUESDAY

Eh! gently for heaven's sake: a bit of charity Madame, or at least a bit of honesty.

—Molière

20

FREEDOM FROM FILTH CAMPAIGN
TO BE TESTED AT TRIAL

The case of *The Société for The Preservation of Christian Morality Against Contemporary Indecency* vs. *Charles Durand* is scheduled for hearing at 2 p.m. today before the Hon. Roger Remonde, Judge of the Thirteenth Precinct Court of Paris.

Though less than a week old, the Durand case has already become a cause celebre throughout France.

The defendant, M. Charles Durand, of Durand's Bookshop and Bindery, No. 12 Street of the Seven Angels, was apprehended in a citizen's arrest last Wednesday by Madame Adolph Hilhaud, Chairman of the Public Parks and Museums Division of the above-named *Société*.

Mme. Hilhaud alleges she caught the defendent seated on the thigh of a statue known as *The Reclining Diana* in the foyer of the Breville Museum, and further that the defendant was in the act of defacing and otherwise marking with lewd, lascivious, immoral and obscene words and phrases in pencil on the abdomen and hip of the prized marble statue.

Upon M. Durand's denial of guilt and refusal to pay a penalty, charges were brought against him by the *Société* and the defendant demanded a public trial.

Mile. E. Mailleferre, of Mailleferre's Religious Arts Shop, No. 8 Street of the Seven Angels,

President of the *Société* stated: "We, of the *Société*
welcome the opportunity of presenting our case to
the decent citizenry of Paris. We feel that such
groups as ours have a perfect right, indeed a duty, to
do everything in our power to survey such places and
to act as guardians of decency. We have nothing
against M. Durand personally, nor do we wish to cur-
tail anyone's freedom of action or expression. But
such acts of gross immorality must be stopped if our
youth is to grow up in an atmosphere cleansed of
filth. It might be added that, the said M. Durand,
who protests his innocence so brazenly, had categor-
ically refused, on the very morning of his apprehen-
sion, to cooperate with our *Société* in its campaign
for clean literature. He is the only bookseller in the
entire St. Jacques Quarter who refused to remove
from his shelves books that we consider offensive to
the public morality."

Questioned in his bookshop, M. Durand heat-
edly denied that he had any thought or intention of
defacing the prized marble statue with pornographic
markings. "That would be an adolescent gesture," he
said. He stated that the markings were already there
and that he would fight this type of persecution in
every court of the land, if necessary.

"This is an issue of grave implications," he
observed. "Can a private sectarian group such as
this *Société* dictate to a free citizenry what its morality shall be, what books it shall read, what films it
shall see? There I was in the Musee Breville. I
became fatigued and seated myself for a moment, not
on the thigh of *The Reclining Diana*, as has been
alleged, but rather on the marble pedestal on which
the figure reclines. Immediately this woman pounces
on me from behind a curtain. This is very grave.
Shall a free citizenry be spied upon by women hiding
behind the drapes of our public museums? I want
this cleared up in a court of law. Those who now
despise me will someday thank me for fighting for
our freedoms."

Concerning his refusal to cooperate with the *Société*'s Decent Literature Campaign, the defendant explained:

"Two women called at my shop early Wednesday morning with a list of books which they said the *Société* found objectionable for one reason or another. They requested that I remove all copies of these works from public sale. It was more or less a blackmail approach. They said that if I complied, they would present me with a cardboard plaque as a cooperator and that if I refused, I would be named in the parish newspaper as a non-cooperator, which would of course seriously damage my business and my personal reputation. Their list was so long that had I complied I should have been left with a shop full of bare shelves. Look at these titles: such things as the admirable *La pesante journee*, Chardonne's *Vivre a Madere*, a classic; even Mauriac's *The Eucharist*, not to mention all of Gide, all of Moravia, all of Colette and Simenon . . . well, the list is endless, and it comprises most of contemporary fiction. To make such works unavailable would be to deprive humanity of contact with almost all of our major artists."

M. Durand remarked that if these works were obscene, then he concluded with St. Paul that those who regard them so are themselves of an obscene turn of mind.

The Durand case has enjoyed wide press coverage, and a large crowd of interested spectators is expected to attend today's trial.

Mademoiselle Mailleferre applied glue to the top corners of the disgusting clipping and pasted it, along with all others in the *Société* scrapbook as part of their permanent record.

Bells clanged out over the snow-covered rooftops to announce nine o'clock Mass at the Dominicans' chapel across the street. It was time to open her shop. Mademoiselle glanced about the salon to see that everything was ready for this morning's special strategy meeting of the *Société*. She dipped her croissant in a bowl of café-au-lait and hurried to finish her breakfast.

21

Durand eased the door closed behind him and shuffled snow from his shoes on the entrance-hall mat. It took a moment for his eyes to accustom themselves to the somberness after the outside brilliance of sunlight on snow.

He heard the noise of a saucer being placed in the sink behind the curtained entrance of the concierge's cubicle, and began to walk quietly across the checkerboard parquet of the vestibule. He did not want to see her. One no longer knew who were one's friends, and after the snubs and glares he had received all over the quarter these past few days, just one more would be too much.

"M'sieu . . . Psst," he heard when he had almost reached the stairs. He sighed, shifted the batch of newspapers from one arm to the other and waited.

"Ah . . . dear M'sieu," the concierge said drawing the words out and flowing toward him in a stooped position with her hands out-stretched in a gesture of pity and pleading.

Durand offered her his free hand in a quick handshake. "You are a hero," she announced with fervor. "You are standing up for the rights of all us citizens of France."

"If only you knew," he muttered.

"Pardon?" she asked, blinking. She reached up to brush croissant crumbs from her wrinkled cheek.

"Nothing, dear friend," he said, for he cared little this morning about the sequence of endearments since it was his attention to such things that had got him into this predicament.

"Those monstrous women," she groaned. "Ah, M'sieu— let me be one of your witnesses. I could tell them about the real Durand, the kind of man I know you to be. And I could provide so much dirt on those sancti . . ."

"You know something about them?"

"Know? Who needs to know? A concierge can tell you shocking things about all women, M'sieu."

"We'll see. I must go upstairs. Has Montausier arrived?"

"A moment ago. I let him in."

As Durand turned, she patted him on the forearm and whispered, "Courage, M'sieu. . . ."

He mounted the stairs slowly, depressed by the caged gloom of the stairwell. At the landing he sniffed a faint cold odor of the bread he had baked last night. He stopped to listen to the voices inside his apartment.

"And the reputation of my poor Helene," Mama's voice lashed out. "What about my own reputation?"

"Madame, please try to understand," Montausier cut in impatiently. "This is far more important than you appear to think."

"Humph."

"It's not merely this matter of poor Durand's being accused of marking the statue—it's the principle of a sectarian group trying to dictate not only the morals of their own people, but of those of others faiths and beliefs as well. Unless they are stopped, there's no telling how far they'll go in depriving us of our freedoms. I tell you, Durand has got to fight it."

"Well, someone's got to take a hand in curbing immorality. If our police won't do it, then groups like this have a prefect right to protect us from *smut*. And I, for one, am going to join them."

"Then you, too," Montausier said in a voice suddenly gentle, "are in favor of this sort of compulsory fulfillment of the Kingdom of God?"

"Well, of course," Mama said flatly.

"I see. But isn't it true that God created man with a free will?"

"Absolutely."

"Why? Wouldn't it be because God wanted man to come to Him of his own free choice, because He wanted man to choose to act virtuously?"

"Of course."

"Isn't it true that the only act which has any virtue in God's sight is a freely-given act?"

"Now, if you're trying to back me into a corner, you're just wasting your . . ."

"No, no, Madame," Montausier said blandly. "I was just examining your idea. Look, suppose you pass a poor beggar-woman on the street. You are moved to charity for one of God's unfortunates, so you stop and give her a coin. You have freely chosen to help her. Do you think this is pleasing to God?"

"Well, naturally," Mama said, exasperated.

"You're absolutely correct. No one would argue that. But suppose you pass this same poor beggarwoman and are moved to contempt. You would never give her a coin. However, this time I'm walking with you. I know that it is virtuous to give alms to the poor, that this is part of the fulfillment of God's Kingdom. So, I put a gun to your head and force you to give her money. Do you think your good act has any moral value in God's sight?"

Durand pressed his ear against the door and listened to the silence as Mama sighed and did not deign to answer.

"It has no value at all," Montausier explained, "because you did not freely choose to do it. You committed a good act because I compelled you to and not because of any good and noble motive on your part. You see, Madame, the fulfillment of God's Kingdom on earth can never be compulsory, simply because such fulfillment depends on man's free consent, on his free gift of himself. The moment I compel you to act virtuously, God is no longer in it, since no act which is 'un-free' has any value in His sight. As for my forcing you to do this good thing—what right did I have to place you under such compulsion?"

"None at all," Mama snapped.

"You're right. I was a private citizen compelling you to fulfill God's Kingdom. Don't you see that this *Société* is trying to do the same thing, only they are six where I was one. I was a dictator and they are dictators in the same sense. Such a dictatorship is the logical alternative to being governed by God. That's exactly where your *Société* errs, even though it deludes itself into thinking it is working in God's name."

"Well, I still say we have a right to be protected from *filth!*" Mama insisted loudly. "You can't get away from . . ."

"Why, I knew you would still say so. And you might have a point if you had any concept of what filth really is. The trouble here is that you and your kind see as filthy a great many things that God obviously created as good," Montausier said with disdain. "So your presumptuous definition of what constitutes filth has no validity whatsoever. You would end up harming yourselves and those whom you seek to protect as much as you harm and disgust the rest of us. In good conscience, I choose to oppose you, Madame."

"Well—you just go right ahead, you old . . ."

"Mother," Helene reprimanded.

"Well, how he can say it's not filthy to sin against God's commandments on purity, or to lead others into impurity?"

"Since we are on God's commandments, Madame, what about the Eighth? Thou shalt not bear false witness . . ."

"What about it?"

"Strange that a group acting in God's name should feel

themselves justified in committing a grave sin against the
Eighth Commandment in order to save us from the harm of the
Sixth? That's what this saintly group has done—destroyed
Durand's good name, born false witness against an innocent
man. Ha! It doesn't make sense."

"Well, I'm not a theologian."

"That's obvious. Neither are they, which is one more reason I don't want them choosing what I shall see and read, or
how I shall act."

"But they have a priest advisor, Father Trissotin. I dare
say he knows a thing or two about theology," Mama said triumphantly.

"That's right. He knows a thing or two. That's hardly
enough, is it? He does nothing but spout the platitudes of the
seminary."

"You, a Catholic, talk like that about a priest of Father
Trissotin's stature. You ought to be ashamed."

"It's hardly a secret, Madame, that not all priests are
theologians."

"Father Trissotin even writes books, and you say . . ."

"He write pamphlets, Madame, full of Goodgoderies and
Sweet-Jesuseries, and probably accomplishes a lot of good if
one has the stomach to read that sort of thing."

Durand opened the door and stepped into the apartment
where an odor of coffee assailed him as though aimed on the
beam of Mama's glare—an odor of unmasked contempt.

He carried the newspapers down the hall to the salon and
dropped them on the couch. Both Montausier and Helene followed him in, but he heard the door slam behind Mama and
her heels club the stairs.

"That was a fine argument," Durand said to his friend.

"It never has entered her mind that you didn't do this
thing," Helene said quietly. "She's convinced you're guilty."

"What about you?" Durand asked. He eased himself into
the lumpy chair where Mama habitually sat and restrained
himself from pulling his pants legs up to the middle of his

thighs in imitation of her.

"Ah," Helene smiled, "you ask me that? Surely you're not serious."

"Do you have that list of books the women brought you last week?" Montausier asked.

"Right here," Durand said, reaching into his inside coat pocket.

"I'll get you both some breakfast," Helene said.

The odor of heating coffee now smelled friendly to Durand.

"Tell me," Montausier said with his eye on the kitchen door. "I've been all over that damned statue. Now, if I'm going to represent you at the trial, you've got to be honest with me. I have to know."

"I wrote on it all right," Durand said wearily. "But nothing obscene. "

"The only thing I found on it that wasn't obscene was something about "dear friend, dear-dear friend, dearest friend."

Durand looked balefully at Montausier.

"You wrote that?" Montausier asked. He broke into laughter as Durand nodded affirmation.

"Why in the hell didn't you say so? Why, that's nothing to . . ."

"Give it a thought. Was a man likely to write that list to remind himself of where he was with his wife?"

"Ah," Montausier nodded, his eyes softening with understanding. "I see . . . Who?"

"The concierge downstairs," Durand admitted abjectly. "On the right thigh I was going to put a list for Madame Carnot, but I couldn't very well admit that, now could I?"

"That old hag? Surely you're not that desperate. Why you gave Flamart and me the impression that half the women of Paris were just aching to give you . . ."

"No—it was something to give her a thrill."

"One of your little projects to gladden the hearts of the aged?"

"A kindness, really."

"I don't doubt it—a heroic kindness, my friend, considering the looks and appeal of this woman."

"And I pay for it heavily, eh?"

"What a strange man you are," Montausier said, as though he only now perceived something of the intimate life of his friend.

"But tell me—why did you make your list on the thigh of that statue?" Montausier sallow face reddened with the force of his contained amusement.

"I don't know. It seemed fitting somehow. Poetic. How was I to know that fire-eating warrior of Christ was there hiding behind a curtain?"

Montausier's laughter cackled forth uncontrollably. "It's too rich, too rich, just the same. My poor old man. Why, you're another Dreyfus."

Durand raised a pained gaze to his friend. "It's ridiculous, eh? But not so funny when people stare at you in the street like you were a child-rapist or worse."

"I know. But we'll prove your innocence."

"Not by admitting what I did," Durand hedged.

"No, by making them prove your guilt. The statue is covered with writings. Let them show which ones are yours. We'll turn their charge into an absurdity. All the newspapers are for you since you refused to throw out the books the *Société* banned. Now, you just leave it to me. Let's go over everything that happened last Tuesday and Wednesday one more time. I think I have a clear picture, but we don't want any loose ends. I'll get together with old Flamart as soon as he finishes at Madame Culuhac's."

"Is he at her place now?"

"Yes. He was afraid the trial might not be finished in time for tonight, so he's making a morning call. By the way, I suppose you've heard that Madame Culuhac's place is their next project."

Durand nodded his head slowly in despair. "They're a

real menace, aren't they? I've never favored such places, but still . . ."

"Why?" Montausier asked. "I've always wondered. You're not fastidious. You like to get yours wherever you can."

"I don't know. I think it happened when I was a youngster. I got a crush on a cousin—my first great love. We petted and even kissed on the mouth—all very pure and beautiful. Her dad, my uncle, saw what was going on. He gave me some money and told me to go to whores. He didn't want me deflowering his daughter, he said. The idea that he'd think our beautiful affair was nothing more than that. I've never been able to bear the thought of going to whores since."

Helene entered with a tray and the two men returned quickly to discussing the books the *Société* wanted Durand to remove from sale.

22

Madame Culuhac held the curtain to one side and gazed down into the street. Flamart was taking a long time back there. A peculiar silence had settled over the house where reflections of sunlight on snow obliterated shadows and made the rooms luminous even in their furthermost corners. She looked at the ribbon of new snow, marked only by Flamart's bicycle tracks, angling up from the Boulevard St. Jacques.

Down the block a group of women gathered before the door of the Religious Arts Shop. Madame Culuhac lifted the curtain higher and pressed her cheek against the glass's coldness to see that they waited for a tall, black-cassocked priest who hurried across to meet them. Handshakes were exchanged and all entered the shop together.

Madame asked herself if she were not looking down on her doom, the final chapter of her poor career. She thought it poignant that it should be so undramatic in appearance. A

group of tiny black figures far below there in the snow, given
the allure of an exquisitely painted miniature, static and wordless—the picture of her ruin.

For it seemed that a Monsieur Aurey had laughingly
mentioned it to Flamart, who had worriedly mentioned it to
Montausier that the *Société* suspected her place of being something more than a mere Massage Emporium, and that they
intended to get the proof and close her down. This was to be
their next major project. Madame Culuhac appreciated
Montausier's warning her. The old fool was solid after all. But
he had been able to offer no satisfactory advice as to how she
might prevent the *Société* from getting the necessary evidence
to prosecute her. All they needed to do was have some spy
come in, make a pretense of getting his treatment, and then
swear that prostitution was practiced there.

Whom could she trust? If dear old Ponneger were alive,
he would on the one hand support the *Société* and on the other
keep her alerted as to their plans against her. But as it was, she
had no good friend in the enemy camp, and had to do battle
with her eyes closed. Why, the very next man who came in
might be their tool.

Care? Caution? To what avail? They'd probably send
some disguised police officer and he'd be the last one she'd
ever suspect of being on the side of the Christians, and she'd
get caught flat in *flagrant delecti*, as she called it technically.
And then wouldn't it be a simple enough matter at her age to
pay all of her savings in fines, or go rot in some prison for violating the Edict of '46.

She saw it all fading, and indeed the view of the mean-
dering little street, the first floor shops across the way, the second and third story red brick apartments, ancient but substantial, with their steep slate roofs covered with snow and
their dormer windows and their little iron balconies blurred
through starting tears.

Dabbing her nose with a handkerchief she sank into her
desk chair. A gentle melancholia detached from the ledger of

past years. How many names of girls and men? Someday
before the end came, she must go through and make a list of all
the girls Flamart had known there. It would make a nice sou-
venir for him. His list would certainly be the longest of all her
clients. And then probably the next longest would be the late
Ponneger's—he, too, a Tuesday night regular. Bless his heart.
He was as undemanding as Flamart except that he always pretended to loathe every moment of it. He was one of those high-
er-class ones who believed the sin was less if one refused to
enjoy it. With him it was strictly a matter of *la sante de l'or-
ganisme*, as he called it.

What was his reason for frequenting her place rather
than having his wife take care of it. Oh yes, it was because
Madame Ponneger believed that it was a deepening thing to
abstain and that if they joyfully faced together the challenge of
overcoming his animal passions, their sacrifice of the things of
the flesh would bring them both to a clearer knowledge of the
things of Jesus. Of course, that was it, for hadn't she subse-
quently made a number of amiable references to the progress
of their knowledge of the things of Jesus?—to have him answer
that they were puttering along more or less and that personally he felt less a gourmand than his wife for such knowledge,
though one had, of course, to respect such spiritual flights.
Then, as though to justify his lack of total cooperation, he
would add that quote from La Rochefoucauld, "If we succeed
in overcoming our passions, it is more because they are weak
than because we are strong," until every girl in the place knew
the maxim by heart and used it to good effect on some of their
more remorseful clients. And now—irony—Ponneger's own
widow was one of the leaders of the *Société* bent on destroying
the very establishment that had been such a solace to him.

And if she went to see Madame Ponneger, showed her the
ledgers to prove that her husband had been only partly
abstemious of the flesh—would that not jar the wind out of
her? An ignoble idea. And anyway, from what one heard about
Widow Ponneger, such a threat would only make her mission

that much more gloriously challenging and to hell with her husband's memory. God, that showed you the difference. Someone could come to her with a threat of dishonoring her own Albert's memory and she would rip out her heart to save his good name.

23

Durand's footsteps crunched in the snow up the Street of the Seven Angels. He inhaled the blue sharpness of the shadowed air and glanced upward to the rooftops where the sun outlined snow dazzlingly against a cloudless sky. The vigorous aroma of wheat bread rose to his nose from the sack he hugged in front of him.

He stopped before the door of No. 5, asking himself if he would still be welcome. Much had happened since his first visit last Wednesday when he had left the bread with one of the friars. The Dominicans had certainly heard the stories of his alleged crime. They might be embarrassed if anyone saw him enter their premises. Well, he would just leave the bread inside and hurry away.

The door opened at his touch and he stepped into the long entrance hall. It was darker and colder than the outside, and filled this time with intonations of Latin. He stepped quietly past the door of the small, box-like chapel where he glimpsed lighted candles and a priest at the altar.

"Monsieur?"

Durand turned, startled. "I was just leaving some bread," he applogized as though caught in a crime.

"Ah yes," the boy said with an expression of sudden delight so intense Durand mulled back over his words to find the source of such joy. The friar took the sack and sniffed into it.

"Mass will be over soon," he said with a soft Spanish

inflection. "If you will kindly follow me."

"Where?'

"Here—to the parlor." The sack crackled with each step the friar took. "You are Monsieur Durand?'

"Yes, but . . ."

"Father Gregoire told me to look for you. I am Friar Lupe. He wishes to thank you for this great kindness. He was gone to take me to the doctor last week when you came. There—please sit." He pulled a chair from the table and turned it into the room.

Durand's hand moved to his coat pocket for a cigarette but he caught himself and allowed it to fall back into his lap. The novice's black eyes glanced about the room and he walked to a small armoire behind the door.

"If Monsieur wishes to smoke." He placed a blue ceramic ashtray on the table near Durand's elbow.

The friar's dark face altered again from an expression of solemnity to a brilliant smile. "I tasted your bread last week," he said timidly. "I had heard Father Gregoire tell that you are a great baker. And I think you are."

"You like the wheat bread, eh?" Durand smiled.

"It is the best I ever yet tasted. It takes care of hunger."

"I'm glad. I'll keep bringing it. Are you the ill friar Father Gregoire was telling my wife about?"

"Yes. Now I'll take this to the kitchen and Father Gregoire will join you."

After a time, the squeak of a shoe approached with measured slowness down the hall. Durand snuffed out his cigarette and turned his attention to the door with a brief upsweep of tenseness. The large figure of a monk entered, full-faced and faintly smiling.

Durand supported himself with his hand flat on the table and rose to his feet.

"Monsieur Durand? I'm Father Gregoire," the monk said as the two shook hands. "Sit down, please. Sit down. I wanted to thank you for the bread."

"It's nothing," Durand mumbled.

"I must apologize for delaying you."

"That's all right," Durand said, disconcerted that a man with the brute face of Father Gregoire could have eyes that were as guileless as Lupe's, no longer with the innocence of ignorance but with the innocence of a man who could be stripped of all illusions and yet suffer no disillusion.

"How's your family?"

"Fine," Durand said.

The same sudden smile of intense pleasure he had remarked on the friar's face now burst over the monk's.

"You know who I am, don't you?" Durand asked uncomfortably.

"Of course

"Do you know the trouble I'm in?"

"Oh, yes . . . goodness," the monk said easily. "My condolences. I know it must be painful for you."

Durand felt his face grow slack with surprise at the monk's expression of sympathy. This great peasant looked at him with no hint of condemnation whatsoever.

"We've followed this with much interest," Father Gregoire said. "If the newspaper accounts are correct, then you are to be thanked for saying some wise things about banning books. I'm afraid our now famous *Société*, like most such groups, makes up in zeal what it lacks in wisdom and prudence."

"But I thought you'd be on their side," Durand said.

"Why?" the monk asked in astonishment.

"Well, because they're Catholics. They have a priest leading them. . ."

"We can sympathize with their ideals—at least we could if we had any clear idea of what they are," Gregoire laughed. "But we still lament their methods. We think with horror of what would happen to the sum total of the world's literature and art if they had their way. But we don't think they'll ever have it. Such groups are always self-defeating."

"I'd like for you to know," Durand hesitated, "that I did not write any obscenities on . . ."

"Please, Monsieur Durand," Gregoire interrupted. "You don't need to defend yourself to me. I'm sure you didn't."

"Tell me, does that Spanish boy know about all this mess?"

"Oh, I'm sure he doesn't. The novices have little contact with the world during this period of their training. It wouldn't make any difference if he did know."

"You think not?"

"No—because—well, in a place like this a man is brought face to face with so many of his own deficiencies, his own imperfections, he's not going to cast any first stone at anyone. If he knew about your embarrassment, it would only increase his sympathy for you."

"I hope he enjoys the bread."

"He does. And it's important for him now. He needs the best nourishment we can provide to keep his strength up."

"I heard he'd been sick. Nothing serious, is it? He seems well. . . ."

"He's terminal."

Durand felt stupefaction numb his brain.

"It's not possible. . ."

"That's how I felt," Gregoire agreed. "He's had this cough—what we thought was a bronchitis. He was so afraid it might be the climate and he might be sent away if we consulted a doctor. So we kept putting off looking into it, hoping he'd get better. But last Tuesday night he had such a bad spell we called the doctor. We had x-rays taken. His lungs are eaten up with carcinomatosis."

"Isn't there anything you can do?"

"Nothing now. We'll let him stay on here. . . ."

"But he's such a youngster," Durand said heavily.

"Yes. The doctor says such carcinomas are rare in one so young."

Durand looked sadly into the superior's eyes and felt

that he had known him forever.

"Are you going to tell him?" he asked.

"I only got the final reports this morning. I told him then."

24

"Is there any further old business?" Mademoiselle Mailleferre asked.

"Not unless you'd happen to have a old cup of tea wasting away," Father Trissotin suggested. "I really apologize, but I rushed right over from Mass, so haven't had anything for breakfast yet."

"Oh, of course, Father," Mademoiselle commiserated. "Why didn't I think of that before?"

The other women rose and offered to fix the priest some tea.

"Well—you've accomplished miracles in one week," he said. "It just shows what concerted efforts of the right sort can do."

"Go on, Father. I can hear you," Mademoiselle Mailleferre called from the kitchen.

"One thing," Father Trissotin said in a louder voice. "I felt I might call to your attention purely as a preventive measure. As you know, the newspapers are taking strong partisan sides, particularly the literary ones, and there are some who will exaggerate as much as possible the content of your statements to the press. I thought it was admirable that Mademoiselle Mailleferre stipulated we have nothing against Durand the *man*, but only against his acts. All of Paris is looking toward us, so—without ceding an inch—we must nevertheless exercise great care to comport ourselves in an impeccably Christian manner. Each of us represents not only himself, his group and even his parish, but we are all being stood up to the bright light of public scrutiny as Christians. I hope I am making myself clear. Let us all guard against any word or act that might reflect badly on the Faith during this campaign. I hope too," Father said as he leaned forward, rested his elbow on his knee and stared keenly at the group, "that we are all individually praying for this Durand person."

"I remembered him at Mass this morning," Madame Duric said distastefully.

"If we pray for him, we can be sure our perspective will remain truly Christian."

Mademoiselle Mailleferre crossed the room with an enormous bowl of tea and placed it on the table beside Father's chair. Steam hovered above it in the inpouring sunlight. Father looked at it, momentarily startled by its size.

What's he supposed to do, bathe in it?" Madame Ponneger bellowed.

"It's a monk's bowl," Mademoiselle Mailleferre explained with some tartness. "All of the Carmelites and Benedictines use them. Would you prefer a cup, Father?"

"No, this is fine," he placated. "Now, getting back to the other. I hope I haven't given you the impression that any of you have defaulted so far. I just think, particularly in view of our plans to investigate Madame Culuhac's establishment, that we must be forewarned about self-control. Such people can outrage an honest person, and an outraged soul is never a wise one. With Durand, it's different. He's a man and men will seldom stoop to actual nastiness in their . . ."

"That man would stoop to anything," Madame Ponneger interrupted. "Have you seen that disgusting new poster he's put up in his shop window? I've been investigating him. I copied it down." She retrieved a small notebook pad from her purse. "It says: 'An old man said: Judge not him who is guilty of fornication if thou art chaste, or thou thyself wilt offend a similar law. For He who said thou shalt not fornicate, said also, thou shalt not judge.' It's supposed to be from the *Sayings of the Fathers of the Desert,* but I don't believe any father ever said such a thing. Why, the man's incorrigible. The idea of his putting the word 'fornicate' right up there in public for all to see. And if you could have seen how he carried on at the Cine Olympia last week. He even winked at me. I tell you it was the most cynical display of lechery I have ever seen."

"Yes, you told us about it," Father said. "Still the point I wish to make is that men lack a certain *tigerish* quality, if I may call it that, that one is likely to encounter in dealings with women, and especially with women of doubtful morals. I'm not saying that Madame Culuhac is *tigerish*, mind you. That I would not know, obviously."

"Well, obviously," Madame Ponneger interjected.

"Yes. But without judging her or being uncharitable, I do think the chances are good that such a woman might resort to some baseness of opposition, like name-calling, hair-pulling, cursing and so forth. And in the heat of your perfectly normal exasperation, you might be overcome and act against her in kind. What I mean is that the temptation to behave in this manner will be greater than it would if you were dealing with a person of the opposite sex."

Mademoiselle Mailleferre's thin shoulders appeared to become unhinged as they always did when she was piqued about something. She glanced at the others as though to say that it was unendurable for anyone to imply that where a principle was concerned she could be swayed by anything so contemptible as the sexual make-up of her opponent. Was not her very life proof enough of that?

"What I mean," Father explained quickly, "is that our basic natures incline us to be more indulgent with those of the opposite sex." He studied the circle of rigid women, lowered the corner of his eyebrows, lifted the corners of his mouth and gazed sincerely down at his hands. "It's just human nature," he mumbled.

Madame Ponneger reached beside her and hoisted the window to let in some of the cold air. Her forehead beaded uncomfortably though there was certainly little enough heat in the room the way that stingy Mailleferre kept the radiator turned down. With her eyes averted from Father Trissotin, she inhaled the snow-chilled purity and asked herself why it was that priests had to be so disgustingly earthy at times. Perhaps one the Desert Fathers *did* say that thing on Durand's sign . . .

From the corner of his eye, Father Trissotin noticed the flush at Mademoiselle Mailleferre's throat. He reached for his tea and swallowed with slow gulpings of liquid and air, grateful now for the size of the bowl that cut off his view of the women. He secreted himself in its foggy, tea-scented intimacy and wondered what in heaven's name there was about this time, this room and these women that had somehow altered his perfectly sane and sincere admonition into one that had evoked the most glaringly genital overtones in the minds of all present.

"Is there any further old business?" Mademoiselle Mailleferre asked with such revulsion Father was certain that if she had a gavel the table would have been shattered by its accompanying blow.

A gasp from Madame Ponneger caused Father to lower his bowl. She sat heavily, her mouth agape, staring down into the street.

"What in heaven's name would Durand be doing at the Dominicans?" she asked.

The others crowded to the window. Below they saw Durand shake hands with Father Gregoire on the doorstoop of the Novitiate. The monk glanced up to them and spoke to Durand. The bookseller immediately turned and studied the windows. Before the women could duck back behind the curtains, Durand saluted them with a gallant wave of his hand. Then he adjusted two books under his arm and strode down the street while the prior closed the green door.

Father Trissotin felt the women's vague uneasiness, and shared it.

"What's he up to?" Mademoiselle Mailleferre asked.

"Why he's over there trying to turn those Dominicans against us," Madame Ponneger said.

"But that's not possible, is it, Father?" Madame Aurey asked. "Wasn't Savanarola a Dominican? Aren't we doing the same thing he did? They couldn't be turned against us, could they? I mean we're all of the same . . ."

"No doubt Durand was just delivering some books," Father said without conviction.

"But why would they buy books from a smut-peddler like Durand?" Madame Ponneger wondered. "Why wouldn't they buy from some reputable Catholic book-seller?"

Father glanced again at the old building across the street and wondered what had gone on behind that façade during Durand's visit. Everyone knew what the Dominicans thought of irresponsible censorship. If they should express disapproval of the *Société*'s campaign, it would be a formidable embarrassment.

"Any new business?"

"I suggest," Father said "that in view of Durand's visit it might be wise if Mademoiselle President were to call on the Dominicans and solicit their active support of our campaign. That way she can set them straight on any misinformation Durand might have given them. In any event, this will show us exactly what their attitude toward us is.

Despite her protestations that she was unworthy, the group voted to send Mademoiselle Mailleferre to the Dominicans.

"The Chair now recognizes Madame Duric, Chairman of the Literature Division," Mademoiselle Mailleferre said.

"There are," Madame Duric began, "some items of interest in my division. First I have a title to add to our banned books, so if you will please get your copies of the booklist. This is a new book, just published. The title is misleadingly beautiful, I'm afraid: *L'Espoir d'un refuge* by a Monsieur Sykes Johnson."

"An Englishman, I suppose," Father Trissotin said.

"I imagine so. At least it says it is translated from the English."

"I'm always a little surprised," Madame Aurey remarked, when our banned books are by Englishmen. I'm naïve I suppose, but I just never associate pornography with the English."

"You know I feel that way too," Mademoiselle Toulenc said. "I always more or less associate pornography with the Slavs. I don't know why. But never the British."

"They're just as bad as anybody else," Madame Ponneger said.

"If we can please get back to the business at hand," Mademoiselle Mailleferre ordered with a light rap of her knuckles on the table. "We were talking about this book."

"Well, pardon the digression," Madame Aurey said. She exchanged a glance of poisonous significance with Mademoiselle Toulenc who widened her eyes as though to say that Mademoiselle President was needlessly cutting since she got her name in the newspapers.

"The reason for condemning this book—Obscenity," Madame Duric announced. "Now girls, and Father, just let me say this: We've taken all our other titles from various lists of objectionable books. This is the first book I've condemned on my very own. And I'm not sure I did it exactly right. So, if you don't mind, let's discuss it a moment and I want to explain why I condemned it. And then I want you to criticize me. Because that's the only way I can learn."

"Of course," Father said. "Did you condemn the book because it contains obscenity of language or obscenity of ideas? I think we should specify that in our lists."

"Well, now, that's a wonderful idea, isn't it girls? I've certainly learned something there. Thank you, Father. To tell you the truth I don't exactly know whether it's language or ideas. It's about this farmer who's married to a Russian immigrant woman and . . ."

"Oh, my Lord," Madame Ponneger snorted.

"How tiresome," Mademoiselle Mailleferre commented.

"Sounds like Giono," Father said with a derisive groan.

"I suppose you'd say it contains obscenity of ideas," Madame Duric went on.

"I see" Father encouraged. "You mean there are suggestive passages?"

"I found them terribly suggestive—lascivious even. But still there's a point here I'm not just certain about. You see," Madame Duric paused and then continued with quiet dignity, "the suggestive descriptions all concern marital things. I don't know if their being married makes a difference or . . ."

"Marital things can be just as filthy as any other," Madame Ponneger said.

"Actually," Father said, folding his hands under his chin in a meditative gesture, "doesn't it amount to this? Some things which are a natural and normal part of marriage become obscene when brought into the open and shared with the world. The more intimate aspect of marriage, which presumably can be beautiful in private, becomes filthy in public."

"That's a very fine clarification, I should say," Madame Aurey observed in her careful style of speech.

"By that standard," Madame Duric said, "then I would not hesitate to call this work obscene."

"The real standard, if you'll forgive me just one further exploration on this point," Father Trissotin said. "Are these passages capable of eliciting lascivious images and desires— not in a person of your quality, of course—but in the immature and susceptible? That is the question you must always ask yourself."

"Well, now I've certainly learned something else. Thank you, Father. I couldn't read very far in this book because it was apparently going to be offensive all the way through."

"I see," Father mused. "Then you didn't number the exact pages on which the objectionable material appeared?"

"No, was I supposed to? I only skimmed the first few pages."

"I might make a suggestion," Madame Aurey interrupted. "Isn't it just possible that we may be challenged and have to admit that we have condemned books that we haven't read? I'm not saying we will, but it might be wise to read all the books to the end."

"I don't see that at all," Madame Ponneger said. "Anyone can tell at a glance whether a book is decent or indecent. That's all we want to know."

"I think," Father placated, "that the happy mean lies between your two opinions. While there is no need to read on and on in a book that is obviously obscene, it would be a good idea to glance through and list a few sample pages and paragraph numbers, so that if we are challenged we can have them on our lists and be able to say: 'Just look on page so-and-so. Would you want your children to read a book containing such expressions or ideas?' That will give a great deal more weight to our condemnation."

"I'll do that without fail," Madame Duric said, as she reached for another paper. "Now, here is a copy of the letter I have been sending to all authors of our condemned books. Father Trissotin has already approved it, but I would like to read it to the group, and then I want you to criticize it."

"You will please read the letter," Mademoiselle Mailleferre ordered.

"Very well. Here it is."

> Dear _____:
> I am writing you on behalf of The Société for the Preservation of Christian Morality Against Contemporary Indecency about your book, which you will find on the enclosed list of condemned works.
> Our judgment of your book as obscene is based on the test of obscenity laid down by Chief Justice Verole, who defined it as anything capable of inciting the young, the weak and the susceptible to immoral desires or acts, or in any way depraving those whose minds are open to such influences and into whose

hands such a work may fall.

Our campaign is working to curb evil literature and further good reading. The people of our nation highly prize liberty, and that is most commendable. Our clean literature drive does not infringe anyone's legitimate liberty, but seeks to prevent a wrong exercise of liberty that violates the rights of others. Undermining morals with obscene words and passages in books does violate, we think you will agree, the rights and liberties of decent citizens. You have only to read in the newspapers and what the psychologists have to say to know that what a man reads influences his actions.

It is our prayerful suggestion that you recall this book from public sale. And we urge you to remember that in order to qualify as clean literature, your future books must be capable of being read in women's groups and by our youth with no possibility of embarrassment or incitement to wrong doing or wrong thinking. Would you be willing to read your book aloud to a large mixed audience?

Hoping that you will give this matter your serious thought and that you will in future works never again be guilty of violating the welfare and rights of your neighbors, we are . . ."

Madame Duric folded the letter slowly against her chest. She waited in silence for the group's reactions.

"Why, I think that's wonderful," Madame Aurey commended. "They know we mean business and yet it is not uncharitable."

"Just the right tone there," Father Trissotin added.

"Have any of these letters been mailed yet?" Mademoiselle Toulenc asked as she reached for the ledger. "We'll need to keep track of the cost of the postage."

"The stationary won't cost anything," Madame Duric said. "Madame Aurey contributed an entire box of her fine Waverly stationary to the cause."

Madame Aurey smiled quietly and nodded her acceptance of the group's implied gratitude in a way that made Mademoiselle Mailleferre wonder if this weren't really a triumphal little dig at the *Société* for its refusal to accept her suggestion that they call themselves the Waverly Anti-Pornographic Society—of all the ridiculous names!

"For the stamps," Madame Duric said, "thirty-seven of these letters have been mailed."

"Any answers yet?" Madame Ponneger asked.

"Two," Madame Duric sighed.

"Well, how were they?" Madame Ponneger asked.

"Rather insolent, I'm afraid."

"Well, I think the group should hear them," Madame Ponneger said.

"Very well." Madame Duric selected neatly-typed note from her sheaf of papers. "The first is from no less a personage than Marechal."

"This is the author of *The World, the Flesh and Father Lefevre?*

"The same."

"You will please make known to us the contents of Monsieur Marechal's letter," Mademoiselle Mailleferre said.

"I will read through without pause."

Mesdames,

I appreciate your kind letter of the 24th. Your denunciation obviously stems from my treatment of sex in my works. I know the mentality of such groups, having dealt with them in Ireland and America. In truth you consider sex to be synonymous with sin, even when it is a treated as a source of virtue, as God obviously intended it to be.

You ask if I would read my book out loud to a large mixed audience. Would you read any Moral Theology textbook out loud to a large mixed audience? Of course you would not. But I am sure you do not brand Moral Theology texts as smut.

I have never written a sentence in any of my books without being certain in my conscience that it could

not offend God. Since receiving your letter, I can only
deduce that God Himself would appear to be far less
restrictive than those who take it upon themselves to
act in His name.

— Marechal

"A most distasteful letter," Father Trissotin said.

"I don't care what he says," Madame Ponneger
announced. "I still say that wherever you find sex, you're sure
to find smut."

"At least in literature," Father amended.

"That's what I mean."

"I don't think his letter rings sincere at all,"
Mademoiselle Mailleferre said. "That part about the moral
theology textbook. I resent his ridiculing the practices of the—
of my—Faith."

"Well, he's Catholic, too," Father Trissotin put in gently.
"He's another one of those writers with the Thomist viewpoint.
It's very difficult to argue with those people."

"Thomists are terribly liberal, aren't they, Father?"
Mademoiselle Mailleferre asked.

"Some do carry it too far. They follow Aquinas's concept
that since the Faith is the One Truth, then no truth discover-
able in science or nature can be in ultimate contradiction to it;
and again that nothing deducible from the Faith can be in
ultimate contradiction to truths of science or nature. Even
though the Church honors St. Thomas as the supreme teacher,
this is a tricky viewpoint that can lead to all sorts of excesses."

"I see," Mademoiselle Mailleferre said. "Now, Madame
Duric, will you read the second correspondence?"

"I will read through without pause."

Christian Ladies,
    My gratitude for your amusing letter about my
books, two of which won the Prix Goncourt for
Literature. I appreciate the details you offer of your
high motives in this campaign for the sterilization of

literature. I admire especially your willingness to
make works unavailable to adults on the grounds that
these works might hypothetically harm the young, the
weak and the susceptible. By this criterion, as Judge
Savante once pointed out, we would have to close
down all printing presses since it is conceivable that a
susceptible moron has the intellectual level of a child's
library. I thank God that you find my books objectionable in this frame of reference.

— Tristan Goudimel

P.S. Tristan Goudimel is, of course, not my real
name, but only a pen name I use in order to maintain
my own private life under my real name. My true
name, known hitherto only by my publishers, is
Guillaume Smut. I am of Alsatian extraction."

"I'd sure like to answer that smart aleck," Madame
Ponneger said.

"I guess we might as well expect that sort of reaction,"
Madame Hilhaud said. "I'd rather hoped for a more pliant
attitude, especially on the part of Christians like Marechal. I
never heard of this Goudimel person . . ."

"Well, he lectures a great deal," Father Trissotin said.
"In fact he is to lecture in this area sometime next month. He's
essentially a poet, though," Father added, as though that
explained everything. "His most famous book is called *La
Boue*. You must have heard of it."

"Wouldn't you know it," Madame Ponneger said. "What
kind of filthy mind would write a book called *Mud*?"

"He also wrote one called *Nostalgia for Paradise*,"
Madame Duric informed the group, after glancing at her list.

"I think we ought to go to his lecture, as a group, and
protest against his being allowed to speak in public," Madame
Ponneger proposed.

A babble of excitement rose from the ladies.

"Do you mean we should picket him?" Mademoiselle
Mailleferre asked.

"Absolutely. We might even check on his life and pass out leaflets at the lecture—let them know the kind of man they've come to hear," Madame Ponneger said.

"Interesting," Father Trissotin said. "We might send letters to his sponsoring group. If we protested with sufficient vigor, they'd at least think twice before another lecturer of Monsieur Goudimel's, pardon, Monsieur Smut's smutty propensities."

"It's this kind of action I've been hoping for from our group," Mademoiselle Toulenc interjected.

The ladies voted unanimously to launch an investigation of the writer's life and to be prepared at his lecture to distribute mimeographed copies of their findings.

"What if we don't find out anything reprehensible?" Madame Aurey asked.

"You can find out something reprehensible about any man if you dig deep enough," Madame Ponneger assured her loudly.

The creaking stairs attracted their attention.

"It's that girl I have helping me downstairs," Mademoiselle Mailleferre apologized. "Honestly, she can't so much as sell a scapular without having to come up and discuss it with me."

Father Trissotin clicked his mouth in sympathy.

"Come on, Claudine," Mademoiselle Mailleferre called. "Hurry up if you want to talk to me. We're in the middle of a meeting."

25

The jangle of his shop door bell caused Durand to look up over the top of his glasses. His new customer was nothing more than a black silhouette against the brightness of outside snows.

"May I look around?"

"By all means, young man."

Decidedly the publicity was doing him more good than harm. People from the quarter who had never been in before, and even complete strangers, dropped by, purchased a book or two, offered a friendly smile and left him with this tacit assurance that they were still on the side of freedom.

"Call me if you need help," Durand said to his customer.

"Thank you. I surely will."

The bookseller inserted a cord in the two holders at the back of the large lavender poster on which Helene had lettered his latest selection for the series of "Quotes From Great Authors." For the past few days, with Montausier's help, he had selected quotations that reflected the enormous wisdom of his stand against the *Société*. This one, quoting Cardinal Newman, was certainly one of his finest. Durand decided to give it the place of honor in the front window where the Maritain poster had enjoyed a week of conspicuous success. This new one would sell less books than the Maritain, which had caused a run on art items. Half of the inhabitants of the quarter now squinted at people in the cafes and water closets and imagined them as painted by Renoir and Ingres. It had become almost a fad. But in this case, the idealistic principle must take precedence. He would put the Newman in the window and hang the Maritain poster high on the back wall.

"Monsieur?" the customer called.

Durand stood the poster against his desk, absently checked to make sure his fly was buttoned and strode out past bookshelves to the aisle where the silhouette stood tall and thin.

"Monsieur," the young man studied Durand through extremely thick glasses, "I am looking," he grinned, pronouncing with such an affectation that it gave him the air of being a pleasant fop.

"Yes?" Durand said.

"I am looking for something on the subject of marriage,"

he said with his lips pursed unctuously, his eyes half-closed in magnification through his lenses.

"This section contains the more recent titles on marriage," Durand said with a counter-reaction of stiffness, for it seemed likely that the young man would take him into his confidences.

"Is this all?"

"*A Truly Christian Marriage* is doing well these days," Durand suggested.

"Now, Monsieur," the young man said as though he were petulant with Durand for mentioning such a title. He stepped back and frowned pleasantly.

"It is you, the celebrated Monsieur Durand, I suppose?"

"The same."

"I am Jacques Aurey, student at the university.

"Delighted to know you," Durand said.

"And I you." The young man smiled even while wincing from the handshake. "The name is not familiar to you?" he asked tauntingly.

"Ah, you are related perhaps to the lady of the . . ."

Precisely," Jacques Aurey chuckled. "She is my good little mother. Forgive her, Monsieur. She is only one of the minor members. Her poor heart is not in this Decent Literature perversion, of that you can be sure. Nor is mine, nor my father's, who only this week bought a book from you."

"Ah?"

"Yes—you don't remember him?"

"Of course, now I remember. Your father is old Flamart's employer? Yes, I've seen him at the Cafe Zeus, and then he was in here this week—nice man," Durand said.

"You don't resent Mama now, please . . ."

"One has to follow one's inclinations," Durand smiled. My sincerity places me in opposition to these ladies, but I do not doubt their sincerity."

"As they are inclined to doubt yours, alas," the young man said with an expression of profound delight on his face.

"Ah, I encourage mother, but still," he shrugged.

"One has but one mother," Durand sighed.

"Precisely. But, Monsieur, believe me. Mama is not in on this proposition against you at all. No. Her function is that insanely noble one of distributing religious pamphlets in the water closets of the quarter."

"Ah," Durand laughed. "So that's where they've been coming from?"

"You should have guessed, Monsieur," the young man chided. He lowered his head and gazed upward as though he were ashamed of the bookseller. "Papa and I are the distributors."

"Well, I could hardly reach the stalls in the one down on the corner this morning," Durand said and nodded in the general direction of the public urinal at the corner of Boulevard St. Jacques and Street of the Seven Angels.

"A veritable mountain of piety, eh?" the young man beamed. "It is I who did that. I was more than generous."

"I almost pissed in my pants before I could climb over it," Durand reproved.

"Oh I'm sorry. Truly sorry. But you should see what I did to the one down in front of the Cine Olympia."

"Surely you could not have put more?"

"The entire east entrance is blockaded with St. Paul, St. Augustine, and Father Trissotin."

"That's admirable," Durand said in awe.

"In truth, I slighted all of the cafe rest rooms in order to make this grand showing."

The bell jangled with the door's opening. Durand noticed the Aurey boy step behind a bookshelf, obviously not wishing to be seen until he discovered who was entering the shop.

"It's the postman, if you'll excuse me," Durand said and hurried to the front of the shop.

"A not-bad load of mail for you, my friend," the postman announced. He handed Durand a double handful of letters. "A new poster, eh?" he observed. "So true, too."

"I have a great new one going up in a few moments," Durand promised as he shuffled the letters quickly between his hands.

"Good. Something piquant, like the Voltaires you used to have, I hope," the postman said. "Well then, till tomorrow."

Durand lifted a letter with a Dijon postmark from the stack and walked back to his desk. "You'll pardon me, Monsieur," he said as he tore open the envelope. "A letter from my son."

"I'll browse," Jacques Aurey said.

Durand unfolded the letter and read:

> Dear Papa,
>   I arrive in Paris at 3 Tuesday to be with you in your difficulty. Courage and good luck.
>   Your devoted and loving son,
>   — Julien

The bookseller re-read the letter and thought of his son in conjunction with Friar Lupe. He wondered how he would ever bear it if his Julien were faced with Lupe's death sentence. He shook his head and turned slowly toward the customer. Lord, this Aurey creature was even more a caricature in comparison to Julien and the Spanish lad. And yet there was something about that horrible friendliness of his to which Durand could not help respond.

"This all you have on marriage?" he asked.

"I'm afraid it is. Those are the best books on the subject so far as I know."

"I was hoping for something a bit dirtier," the youth said glumly.

"But, Monsieur—I don't sell dirty books," Durand protested, suddenly suspicious.

"You don't trust me," Aurey said, closing his eyes sadly.

"Of course, only I really don't sell the kind of books you want."

"You think badly of me now?"

"I assure you I don't. I enjoy them myself, but . . ."

The door's tinkle caused them both to turn in time to a large woman enter.

"Au revoir," the boy said quickly. "Good luck this afternoon. "

"Thank you."

Aurey scooted, bent almost double, behind the bookshelf into a back aisle and darted out the door as the lady walked toward Durand.

"Madame?"

"Monsieur."

Durand squinted against the light. "Is this, by hazard, not Madame Culuhac?"

"But yes," she answered in her perfectly modulated voice.

"Welcome to my shop, Madame. Forgive me for not recognizing you instantly—the sun was in my eyes."

"It is nothing, Monsieur," she said, shaking his hand. "Could I leave these somewhere while I look around?" She held out a sack.

"Of course. Let me take it. Nothing breakable?"

"No—just some figs and prunes for my little supper tonight."

"Very good for the digestion," Durand said, flustered by the pleasure of her visit. He hurried to the back and deposited the sack on his table as though it contained eggs."

"Ah," he said, returning to her and rubbing his thick hands together. "What superbly radiant weather, eh?"

"I adore the snow," she answered with a quiet smile.

"And I also. Could I help you in a selection? Or would you prefer to look around? Take your time, of course."

"I was thinking of some poetry—as a gift you know. Something in good taste, but not too expensive."

"Of course. Right over here. Mallarme, Eluard, Reverdy. Ah, you knew Reverdy just died. Here's his last volume, just in, but frightfully expensive, I'm afraid." Durand drew from the shelf *La liberte des mers* and flipped through the pages.

"Magnificent," Madame Culuhac observed.

"Yes, just look. Illustrated by Braque. Great art and great poetry are not dead in France."

"No indeed—but I could not afford . . ."

"No, no, no—I wasn't trying to make a sale," Durand assured her. "I just wanted to offer you the pleasure of seeing such a volume." He looked closely at a page and read a passage aloud.

"It's very moving. But such sadness," Madame Culuhac said.

"Or is it serenity, Madame?" Durand replaced the book reverently. "Now, what can I show you?"

"I was thinking about Aragon. Such a resonant name. Is he good?"

"A fine poet become middling in my opinion, now that he has allowed politics to . . ." Durand shrugged. "But to tell the truth, Madame, between you and me, I will admit I'm not really fond of poetry."

"My reaction exactly. But still, poetry volumes do make tasteful gifts. Well, just give me something in a moderately handsome edition—a nice binding."

"Then you will want something from the Pléiade collection," Durand said. He reached into a shelf. "Here's a lovely little volume: *The Complete Works of Rimbaud.*"

Madame took the book and opened it to 'A Season in Hell.' She laughed. "It sounds gruesome."

"His masterpiece," Durand said. "Someone has called it a work of 'diamond prose'" he added, repressing a smile and rolling his eyes ceilingward at the richness of the description.

"Really. . ." she said. Her lips moved silently as she read. "It doesn't really make much sense, does it?"

"The great ones almost never do," Durand said. "From what I understand, one must judge them by the degree of impassionment they managed to communicate. One keeps an open mind and more or less goes along with them, you know."

Seeing that his sale was slipping away, Durand stepped close beside Madame Culuhac and pointed with his forefinger to one of the lines. Loudly he read: "Hunger, thirst, shouts, dance, dance, dance, dance!" He glanced searchingly into her face for some reaction. A faint odor of snuff drifted to him. "That evokes something, just the same, eh? It's really powerful."

"Oh yes, no doubt about it, but . . . Oh, I guess I'll go ahead and take it."

Together they walked to his desk and she waited while he wrapped the book. Durand noticed her stand away and bend her body to the side to read the new poster, and he quickly set it upright for her. They admired the bold block lettering:

WE CANNOT HAVE A SINLESS LITERATURE ABOUT SINFUL MEN, AND NOTHING IS BARRED PER SE.

— NEWMAN

"Now there's a man with a head on his shoulders," Madame said. "Who is he?"

"Someone very important in religious things, I judge. I sell an occasional volume of his work. He noticed Madame Culuhac's involuntary grimace of distaste, eloquent evidence of her resentment of the Christians today. They exchanged a glance of understanding.

"In any case," she conceded, "this one has intelligence."

Durand bowed and showed her out, remarking to himself the delicacy of taste she had demonstrated in not mentioning either her own or his difficulties with the *Société* or his trial this afternoon, though her positive reaction to the poster showed him she was fully aware of the situation.

He returned to his desk and glanced down at the open book which Father Gregoire had lent him. It recalled Lupe to the fringes of his thoughts and filled his chest with a clouding heaviness. He seated himself in the quiet sun-radiant atmosphere of his shop and copied the passages he intended to use for new posters to reinforce his stand.

He read the passage by Father Gerald Vann that was printed on a small catalogue card: "There is no book, from the Bible on down, and no work of art that might not be a source of danger to someone at some time."

That was the stroke of brilliance for which he must be grateful to Father Gregoire. Of course the monk had not actually suggested that he use the book in this manner, but only that these ethical studies by the great Dominican scholars might be excellent sources of clear thinking in rebuttal of the *Société*'s arguments for censorship. It permitted Durand to answer the good ladies with quotes from scholars and priests of their own faith. They could toss off others, but these they had to take seriously.

Perhaps he might order a few copies of this book and arrange a window display—or even send complimentary copies to the ladies of the *Société*.

26

With the high clear clangor of the noon bell from the Dominicans, Mademoiselle Mailleferre seated herself at the rear of her store and began putting on her galoshes. Claudine bade her "a good lunch," and rushed out the door.

"Never anxious to get to work," Mademoiselle said as she got to her feet and stumped her galoshes against the floor, "but always anxious to leave."

Opening the door, she was assaulted by the immediate loudness of bells and the impact of freezing sunlight against her face. She picked her way carefully across the street which was now so solidly iced that the footsteps left no imprint in the snow. The large clock-tower bell continued tolling its majestic hours, bronzing the atmosphere, while the smaller bell from the Dominicans rang in syncopation to it, silvering the atmosphere. The two combined in metallic concord to strike a thousand echoes from the frozen snow.

Mademoiselle Mailleferre timed her arrival at No. 5 so that she could not see Father Gregoire about the *Société* until after she had been fortified by her noonday devotions. She hurried into the entrance hall as the bells died away. Her galoshes sucked loudly at the polished floor with each step she took toward the chapel.

Beyond the refectory's open double doors at the end of the hall she watched monks with grey denim aprons over their white robes wheel carts of food, while others stood quietly behind tables. The moist odors of vegetables and boiled meat offended her.

It took her some moments in the chapel each day to quiet the ferment of aversion this place inspired in her. She considered it a part of her cross that she lived opposite the Dominican monks rather than some lovely order of cloistered nuns. Nuns had a certain bloom about them, a quiet radiance that lifted them far above the ordinary, whereas these monks, no matter how holy they might be, looked utterly common. She struggled against her antipathy, telling herself that one could pray in one chapel as well as in another; but this place was so horribly masculine with its stench of men and meat and vegetables and poverty and silence. Nowhere could she detect a hint of the refinement and delicacy of atmosphere which she associated with the things of the spirit.

Dipping her gloved fingertips into the Holy Water, she crossed herself and ended the gesture by bringing the dampness to her lips as she had once seen a Spanish Carmelite do in a religious movie. After her deep genuflection, she proceeded to her regular pew halfway to the front of the empty chapel.

She knelt and gazed toward the red sanctuary lamp that hung on a short chain from the ceiling. The chapel was disconcertingly light with reflections from the outside glare that flooded the room with shadowless brightness.

Mademoiselle fingered her rosary beads through the muffling cloth of her gloves and fretted for the more solemn comfort of those rainy days when the chapel was obscured in gloom and the sanctuary lamp shone as a true light in the darkness.

The racket of pots and pans through the open door of the sacristy to the left of the altar hurt her. Nuns would never hurl things in the kitchen like that, she thought.

After years of making her devotions on schedule, Mademoiselle knew the routine so perfectly that she anticipated to the instant the beginning of the Benediction. A momentary hush preceded it, then many voices in unison rose and fell in the monotonous Latin cadences. The superior's gavel tapped at the end and she heard benches scrape on the floor and the silverware's tinny jangle.

The sole voice of the reader echoed down the corridor from the refectory, half-singing a text to the silently-eating monks and novices. Because of the reader's chanting manner and the distortion of his voice through distance, Mademoiselle could understand only occasional fragments. It was a constant frustration to her to meditate under such a handicap.

Despite herself, she concentrated on the stately and expressionless march of words, hoping they would be a continuation of the story about the nuns of the St. Rose of Lima Order who cared for cases of incurable cancer.

"The words 'soul' and 'mind' do not have the same meaning," intoned the reader, without a trace of interest to color his voice.

The phrase drifted to her with serene detachment, and she felt the timelessness of it—as though she listened to a refectory reading from the Middle Ages or the Sixteenth Century, in a monastery in Spain or Italy or Holland; or from any time or any place out of countless meals taken in cloisters in the past. She felt a vague strangeness to think that she, woman and a virgin, was overhearing centuries of refectory readings in monasteries where no woman had ever been allowed to penetrate.

"A man of refined soul may have an unpolished mind, a vigorous mind may be joined to a feeble soul. . ."

It was going to be another one like that, she sighed. No stories about nuns today. In any case it would do these Dominicans good to hear that, although they might be brilliant and have vigorous minds, it did not necessary follow that they could afford to be complacent about their souls.

Mademoiselle sought to attach herself to the ebb and flow of the words, as a matter of devotion and discipline; even though such things bored her. Mind and soul, what difference did it make for heaven's sake? It was so simple if one just followed the true precepts of Christianity.

"Almost all moral education is based upon a framework set up by the mind which wearies and atrophies the soul," the reader continued.

Mademoiselle's forehead tightened and drew downward in a frown until the blurred fringe of her eyebrows trembled at the upper edge of her vision.

Honestly—was he having the temerity to imply that moral education wearied and atrophied the soul?

"It consists in precepts and maxims of conduct going no deeper than the brain and abandoning the soul to a wretched mechanical interplay of tropism and instinct . . ."

She sat rigid, holding her rosary beads against her chest to prevent their rattling. Were they trying to prove now that morality went no deeper than the brain and that it made the soul wretched? The outrage of the idea became the vaster outrage of having provoked a hidden uneasiness within her. It struck her like some premonition of disaster. She blanked her mind against the bite of its truth. These Dominicans carried their boldness entirely too far. The sides of her hands became aware of the softness of her breasts. She clutched the rosary beads and pressed them hard against her, struggling against her pride in the size of her breasts, casting out the images of love, of nursing, of the whole yearning for motherhood . . . all of it, but God with what pains sometimes, all given up for the love of God.

"And what elaborate deceits we employ to assume a behavior which life repudiates and denounces as artificial!"

Mademoiselle was certain she detected a tone of relish creep into the reader's voice.

Elaborate deceits? One would think this were a house of Satan rather than one of God.

She winced at the roar of her clothes when she shifted positions, for even that was enough to cloud the next phrase. But she understood that it was something about this sort of behavior producing nothing but "dead virtues" born of the mind's rejection of the great gifts of life, while the soul squirmed wretched and decaying beneath them.

The phrase "dead virtues" found inadmissible consonance within her and impelled her against her will toward the door.

"We are duped by our neighbor's shell of devitalized virtues just insofar as we ourselves are seeking a refuge and an alibi beneath them," the reader sang out.

Mademoiselle stopped in her tracks to silence the rubbery squish of her galoshes. God. There was some truth in that. She saw in sudden a blasphemous image of the entire membership of the *Société* wearing uniforms on the pockets of which were exquisitely embroidered the motto: "Shell of Devitalized Virtue." She pushed the door open slightly and pressed her ear against the crack.

"Nothing is more difficult to grasp than the movement in which the mind deserts the soul, leaving it weakened by its absence, and turns back on itself: it comes so naturally to us! In actual fact, how many acts do we perform with our whole soul and our whole being?"

Mademoiselle's frail shoulders drooped slightly and she allowed the door to rankle shut. Was this the reason for her great dryness of soul. How long, she asked herself, how long since she had done anything with her whole soul and her whole being? Was not her countenance a constant supershifting of faces according to the needs of the moments, according to what was expected on the surface, while her heart languished far beneath, untouched in its own private dying? For how long, now, had she acted the role life assigned her—the pious Christian, the militant lover of Christ, the believer who no longer felt, though she still believed?

"The vast majority of men, in the whole course of their existence, attain to plenitude of soul only for scattered moments, quickly fading . . ."

She passed her pew and walked slowly toward the left side of the altar rail where a plaster statue of the Blessed Virgin gazed down on a rack of votive candles in blue glasses at her feet. Some of the candles were lighted and flickered pale.

She stared into the expressionless face of the statue, into its painted eyes and glazed features, and saw in its lifelessness something of her own lifelessness; and in its solid plaster interior something of her interior hardness. But how else could a person like her be? She had elevated herself painfully above striving after the false gods of beauty or love in a world that was all ugliness and lovelessness. What had been left then but to strive for salvation for herself and the world? She rested her elbows on the altar rail.

A hateful phrase by Charles Peguy detached itself from her memory and she closed her eyes against its perception: "Because they love no one, they imagine they love God."

How did one know? No matter how one tried, how did one know? Things that had been clear and important before had now fallen into confusion.

It could not be true. Reality was of the world, a thing to shun, for it brutalized the soul.

Mademoiselle fumbled for the seventh bead of the first decade of her rosary and held it between both hands. Her whispers floated out in vapor almost invisible in the chill white air.

But the prayers would not lift her into cold altitudes. Isolated fragments of the reader's text jarred through like shouts beyond the wall of a dream.

"The distress of modern man, faced with the spectacle of a world becoming more and more recalcitrant to his orders as he extends his apparent dominion over it, has for its origin this unhealthy misunderstanding of the proper function of the soul."

Could she have been that wrong, she asked herself. At least there was doubt—doubt not being born, she realized, but merely being revived from some deep forgetfulness.

"The strange fact is that modern man no longer knows how to feel."

This phrase broke through the encrustations of her piety like a physical blow. Yes, she moved through life without feeling. But so did everyone else, everyone she knew. Since it was average, she had supposed it was normal.

Mademoiselle glanced at her hands in front of her face, so close the rosary beads hazed. She was on the twenty-ninth one—and had no recollection of having prayed at all.

"The soul needs the help of the mind on condition that the mind is the soul's own deepest intimacy." The reader's chanting voice faded to introspective softness before cresting back to strength: "When the mind is enveloped by the soul, then anger may spring from charity, authority from love, action from contemplation. These seemingly irreconcilable qualities, proceeding from the opposite extremes of mind and life, may fuse together in a synthesis that is truly original."

Mademoiselle bent forward and rested her forehead on her folded hands. She listened to the description of herself. Was there a trace of originality left in her? Any feeling? Any spontaneity? Any inconsistency, even? No, it was an automaton existence, forever following rules, forever seeking to reform herself and others.

"In this connection it is significant that the saints are all different from each other, despite their similarities," the reader intoned. "Whereas the routine practitioners of religion are all exactly alike."

The words filled her with revulsion deeper than sickness, but she recognized their truth. Were not she and the other women of the parish, the other "routine practitioners of religion," in fact, exactly alike? Was there anything to distinguish the one from the other?

"Nothing can make one emptiness different from another emptiness," the reader answered with implacable sweetness.

The words were no longer those placidly flowing ones of a human in the refectory. They had become attuned to the coldness, as though emanating from the walls and floor and ceiling, colorless and piercing as ice, and full of contained mystery. She felt it as the chilling breath of God who tossed into her face the image of herself as nothing more than one of the routine practitioners of religion.

"What they all have in common is the construction of a universe, a sheer substitute product designed to complete the interior vacuum induced by the soul's anemia and the mind's aggression . . ."

The words fascinated her as some nightmare from which she recoiled but could not flee. Her legs ached from the stiffening cold that penetrated so thoroughly she felt no warmth left in her body. She remained kneeling, too tired suddenly to resist the pulverizing accuracy of the attack. Removing her gloves, she lowered her head into her hands, aware of all their wrinkles and lines and lye-soap odors, and prayed upward from the dark hole of vertigo, asking God to forgive her the littleness, the fastidiousness of her love, and the greatness of her presumption. In the greenish stipple behind her closed eyelids, she listened for some answer and heard nothing but the distant buffeting on wind. The reader's voice droned on, telling her that it was late, late in her life.

It was not just. Here she had rejected the bricks and stones and lamp posts of the world in her search for spiritual perfection. Here she had rejected communion with hearth's heat and all the appetites of her flesh, and the grass and all things in nature in order to live exclusively in the realm of the spirit. And now the reader told her that she had replaced these things with a vacuum and then been obliged to construct a sheer substitute universe to fill this vacuum. He told her that all of this showed not love of God, but contempt for God's creation—seeing as evil what God created as good. She realized that her mind, divorced from her soul, saw as obscene what her body saw as good and what her heart saw as beauty. The phrase from Marechal's letter to the *Société* returned to her: "I can only deduce that God Himself would appear to be far less restrictive than those who take it upon themselves to act in His name."

Darkness spread behind her closed eyelids. She opened them to find the garish light had faded to somberness in the chapel. The sky must be clouding, she told herself. Blue votive lamps at the statue's feet now cast light on the underside of the folds of the Virgin's robe. She noted the toenails of the feet of the Mother of God, and again on the feet of Christ himself when she looked toward the Crucifix.

She rose to her feet and hesitated. Something was different. She listened. The racket of plates and silverware, the noises of eating had stopped. The sanctuary lamp flickered greater intensity over her head. It was too quiet, too terribly quiet. One would have thought that only she and the wind existed in this world of shadows.

"This reading," concluded the reader mournfully, "has been taken from *Incarnation and Pseudo-Incarnation* by Marcel de Corte."

The expected tap of Father's gavel did not come. Instead, Mademoiselle heard him speak quietly to the novices. "I want to clarify two points from this reading," he said. "First, you must not think that it in any way denies the importance of the mind; it speaks only of the tragedy that occurs when the mind divorces itself from reality, from the soul."

Mademoiselle pushed open the door into the corridor that had become dark as twilight. Looking toward the refectory, she saw the Prior, standing with his back to her as he addressed the novices.

"Morality is not amiable," he said, "and it was never the goal of the saints, but simply a natural consequence of their love for God. Morality as a goal in itself is false. The goal is love of God. Morality will then take care of itself. For the saint, the great keyword is charity, in the sense of St. Paul's admonitions; it is a charity that does not *judge*, that never thinks evil of another. But for the moralist, the keyword is reform, usually in a sense that he thinks evil of everything except himself."

Somewhere beyond her numbness, Mademoiselle heard the sharp tap of the wood gavel, followed by the floor-scraping of monks and novices rising from their benches. She watched Father Prior and the others enter the hall and advance toward the chapel. Each of the rustling white shadows bowed to her before passing through the door. She shriveled within herself, certain they saw through her falsity.

She decided not to bother Father Gregoire with her espionage mission from the *Société*. Opening the door, she stepped outside. The air was scarcely colder than inside. The street stretched somber in that peculiarly artificial light of black skies combined with white snows. Mademoiselle felt herself a stranger to the time and place, yet, under the monochrome thickness of clouds, the world became warmer. Where she had seen only white and gray in the snow an hour before, she now perceived softer blues. Smoke from chimneys across the boulevard, trailing up white against the sky's darkness, no longer represented contemptible weakness, but humanity warming itself within.

Despite the invasion of chill, she stood on the sidewalk and allowed herself to be steeped in this bewildering renovation of the senses, responding to the simplest sights: the mortared seams of brick wall sweeping away to convergence at the building's corner, the worm-pocked wood of the door beneath scaling green paint, the vitreous reflections of the street in her shop windows, as though some inner sight had broken through the caul of outer sight. All sights and sounds and odors entered into the depths of her being, as though her soul were actually uniting with the snow, the bricks, the cars and the smoke, as if she were being fed by them. She submitted to the actions and asked herself if this were the way the world really looked.

27

"Happy to see you back in your robes again, Maitre Montausier," Judge Remonde said as he adjusted his own black silk sleeves.

Montausier, scrupulous to avoid anything that might be construed as currying favor by Maitre Guinder, attorney for the *Société*, nodded politely to the judge and did not speak.

The judge walked out in swishing silks from his chambers toward the crowded courtroom.

"Will you help me with the loop button?" Montausier asked Flamart. He turned his back. "Yes, that's fine."

"That gown makes you look like an abbot," the old man said feebly. "Now, when I get up and you start asking questions, I'm supposed to say just . . ."

Montausier frowned violently toward the stone mason, who reddened beneath his white hair without knowing precisely why.

"You just tell the truth, answer my questions—that's all," Montausier instructed.

He glimpsed a cramp of suspicion on Maitre Guinder's rather youthful and clean-featured face. "Now—is Marthe out there?"

"Oh yes," Flamart said. "She'd not miss a circus like

this, you can be sure."

"Fine. You go sit with her and I'll call you when we need you," Montausier said, walking with Flamart to the door.

Lights had been turned on in the courtroom because of the early-afternoon darkness. Montausier gazed across the room's glare toward gray windows at the far side and saw that snow had begun to fall. The spectators' faces were strangely solemn, as though depressed by the bald lights. He noted that most of them were women of a certain age, undoubtedly with strong sympathies for the *Société*, there to see that their children win the court's protection from filthy influences.

Montausier sniffed the familiar odor of mustiness that always clung over halls of justice, as though a dust storm had blown through a moment before. He walked slowly toward the large mahogany table at which Durand, wearing his finest blue double-breasted suit and with his hair immacultely combed back from its center part, sat in stiff dignity.

"Don't stare at the judge like you were being sentenced to the guillotine," Montausier whispered. Durand shook his head slightly and blinked his eyes as though he did not realize his stare had been fixed on the judge's elevated desk.

"What happens first?" he asked Montausier.

"First I'm going to ask for a dismissal, just to have it in the record. That'll be turned down and then we'll get on with the trial."

They watched Maitre Guinder, the embodiment of confidence, walk toward the table where the women of the *Société* smiled at him. Madame Ponneger made a pretense of applauding their champion.

"Who's he?" Durand asked.

"Maitre Guinder. He's their lawyer. Once studied to be a priest but changed to law. Was a pretty good amateur musician-composer, writes Masses with a Sweet Jesus flavor. Hates filth and communism. Writes a lot in Catholic newspapers, mostly shallow tirades; extremely careless with his logic, but fancies himself a philosopher. He's an amateur theologian and has a real Inquisition mentality. Loves to . . ."

The judge's gavel pounded against the block of wood atop his desk with such sharpness that Madame Ponneger jumped and gasped.

"Do you think there'll be any trouble?" Durand whispered above Judge Remonde's droning voice.

"No—only think before you answer any of Guinder's questions. He's sharp in his own bungling way."

Durand settled back in his chair and watched Montausier rise to present his formal request for a dismissal. His glance drifted toward the ceiling where cherubic and enormously masculine angels flew about among blue skies and pink clouds, their genitals coverd by strips of the most delicate gauze. For a moment Durand wondered if one of the ladies of the *Société* had been in there with paintbrush, assigned to cover the nudity of these infant angels.

Montausier began speaking—but with such quiet dignity Durand was appalled. He glanced toward Helen in a momentary panic. The old fool would never sway the court with that cool and limpid reason of his. Durand had expected a much more dynamic defense, of the type Zola had undertaken on behalf of Dreyfus, with glowering and fist-slamming. Why, the lawyer showed far more spark in their cafe arguments than he showed here in the courtroom.

Judge Remonde rather beignly refused Montausier's lame request and asked the lawyer to call his first witness to the stand.

Making his way past chairs to the witness stand, Durand's heavy jowls sagged and he wondered if he had been foolish, after all, to accept the services of his old friend. But still, Montausier had been a highly esteemed lawyer in his day.

After being sworn in, Durand seated himself in the elevated chair beside the judge's desk. He gazed downward on rows of hostile faces. Judge Remonde fondled his gavel as the room settled into silence.

"Please state your full name," Montausier said.

"Charles Edmund Dantes Durand," he said, watching the aged court reporter type with incredible speed.

"Your occupation, Monsieur Durand?"

"Bookseller," Durand answered.

"Smut peddler," Madame Ponneger answered in an almost inaudible whisper. Judge Remonde glared at her and reached for his gavel. Mademoiselle Mailleferre, reddening in embarrassment, reached over to pat Madame Ponneger's powerful hand in an attempt to silence her.

"Is it correct that on Wednesday, January 30 of this year, at approximately eleven-thirty a.m. you were in the foyer of the Breville Museum?"

"That is correct," Durand answered, prepared for the impersonality of Montausier's questions, but nevertheless offended that his old friend should speak to him as though they had never met.

"Would you, Monsieur Durand, tell the court exactly what you were doing there?"

Durand cleared his throat and assumed an expression of portly innocence that caused Madame Ponneger to twist in her seat in a movement of disgust. He then noticed Mademoiselle Mailleferre lean forward and watch him with a strangely soft expression that startled him.

"It was a foul morning, a rainy and depressing morning. On such days, when business is slow, I often close my shop a few moments early at noon and drop by the museum on my way home to lunch."

"The museum is directly across the street from your store?

"Yes."

"And you often go there?"

"Oh, very often," Durand said, touched now by the reverence with which Montausier addressed him.

"Is this because of your great love for art?"

"Yes, I think there is something about great art that uplifts and refines the soul."

"Does that include all art?"

"Yes—whether it be great music, painting, books, statues or ceramics. Art, as the celebrated Cardinal Newman . . ."

"Objection!" Maitre Guinder interrupted.

Madame Ponneger nodded her agreement of the lawyer's action, though she had no clear notion why he objected.

"Sustained," Judge Remonde ruled. "This court will not admit hearsay evidence."

"Attorney for the defense," Montausier said, "is seeking to establish the defendant's reasons for going to the museum."

"The Court understands," Judge Remonde said. "However, as you well know, quoting from authorities constitutes hearsay evidence unless the authority is in the court to testify. The Court is interested only in Monsieur Durand's reactions to art. Unless, of course, you wish to call this Newman person as a witness. Is he in the courtroom?"

"Cardinal Newman," Montausier explained with exquisite gentleness while he checked Durand's chuckle with a glare, "is dead."

"Oh. . . . Well, the witness will please confine his statements to the facts," Judge Remonde said sharply.

"On the morning in question," Montausier asked quickly, to divert attention from Judge Remonde's embarrassment, "did you have any particular reason for going to the museum, other than the ones you have described?"

"Yes."

"Will you explain this reason?"

"Of course," said Durand. "I had only that morning installed a window display of art books around a poster containing a quote from the great philosopher, Maritain, and . . ."

"Is this the poster you refer to?" Montausier lifted the large cardboard from the table.

"The same."

Montausier showed it to the judge and asked that it be placed in evidence as exhibit A for the defense.

"Please tell the Court why you went to all of the trouble

and expense of preparing such a poster?"

"The idea intrigued me. Maritain's suggestion that we look at people as though they were paintings had, in fact, opened an entirely new world to me."

"And you wished to share that richness with people of the quarter who might pass by and read the poster, is that correct?"

"Yes," Durand said, his attention distracted by Mademoiselle Mailleferre who read the poster avidly.

"This occurred before you were apprehended in the museum?"

"Yes, the morning of the day I was assaulted."

Madame Hilhaud's mouth flew open to protest. "Why I didn't assault him. . ." she said in a loud stage whisper to Madame Ponneger.

"This is not the first time you have displayed such posters for the cultural edification of your fellow man, is it?"

"No, I've been doing that for years."

Judge Remonde glared toward the members of the *Société* and lifted his gavel as Madame Ponneger hissed to lawyer Guinder, "Why don't you object? She didn't *assault* him."

"Order there!" the judge called.

"Objection, your Honor. Monsieur Durand's art philanthropies have no relevance to the case at hand," Guinder said nastily.

Montausier stepped before the judge's desk. "Counsel for the Defense," he said, "wishes to establish the reason why the defendant went to the museum this particular morning."

"Objection over-ruled!" the judge announced.

Montausier faced Durand again. "Will you explain what this poster has to do with your going to the museum on the day in question?"

"There had been considerable reaction from passers-by that morning," Durand said. "In fact, Maritain's idea caught fire in the neighborhood, and I suppose you might say that their enthusiasm rekindled my own. I went across to the museum to study the paintings on the second floor in order to coordinate them to the sentiments of this poster."

"For what purpose, exactly?"

"So that I might, for example, mention to a customer—go over and look at that handsome Delacroix portrait, or that Giotto, and then see how many people in the street or in church look like living portraits by these same artists."

Judge Remonde leaned forward and listened with interest, while Madame Ponneger stared outraged at the other members of the *Société* as though to reassure them that this was the most monstrous lie in the history of French jurisprudence. Her snort was so loud Judge Remonde tapped his gavel lightly.

"If you don't keep your chums quiet," he said to Maitre Guinder, "I'll have to order them to wait outside."

Father Trissotin fixed his gaze on his hands as though to control himself from a more violent reaction to the judge's insolence. Madame Ponneger clamped her jaws shut and stared toward the angel-crowded ceiling.

"Very well, then," Montausier continued. "Am I correct in stating that for the benefit of the entire neighborhood, you went across to the museum around eleven-thirty?"

"That is correct."

"Did you go alone?"

"Yes."

"Aside from Madame Hilhaud, did you meet or see anyone else in the museum?"

"I did see Flamart, the stone mason, briefly when I visited the men's room."

"Anyone else?"

"No one."

"In other words, except for you and the stone mason, Flamart, the museum appeared to be deserted?"

"That is right."

"Please tell the Court what happened after you entered

the museum."

"Well, I was walking through the foyer on my way to the stairs and I passed the beautiful statue known as *The Reclining Diana*."

"Will you give the court your studied opinion of this statue as a work of art?"

"The statue is one of the incomparable masterworks of the Greek era."

"Would you estimate the statue's financial worth?"

"It is priceless, of course."

"Now, will you tell us what happened next?"

"I noticed that there was scarcely a spot on the masterpiece where the virgin marble shone through—so thoroughly was it covered with pencil and crayon markings. I bent down to study these markings."

"Thinking you were alone in the foyer, is that not correct?"

"Yes. I would scarcely have studied them had I known I was being watched. I found them so offensive that I went down to the cellar in search of the janitor, intending to complain about the markings. It's his job to keep the statues clean. I wanted to see this artwork returned to the luster which it rightfully . . . Well in any case," Durand hesitated and glanced toward the ceiling as though he had forgotten what to say next.

"Did you find the janitor?"

"No."

"Did you meet anyone else?"

"Yes, while there I availed myself of the men's room facilities, and it was there I met Flamart."

"Did you enter into conversation with Flamart?"

"Of course—we're longtime friends."

"Very well, what happened then?"

"Not finding the janitor I returned upstairs. I thought I was alone and that it might not look too ridiculous if I were to undertake to clean the statue myself. I was seated on the marble pedestal and was getting ready to erase some of the more

revolting of those lewd marks when Madame Hilhaud flew at
me from behind a nearby curtain. She obviously mistook what
I was doing because she accused me of writing lewd things on
the statue. I, of course, did no such thing."

"Please tell the court what then happened."

"I tried to be pleasant about it, tried to explain what I
intended to do. But she grabbed the pencil from my hand."

"Did she explain why?"

"She said something about it being proof of my guilt, and
that she was making a citizen's arrest."

"Then what happened?"

"Then she went to fetch a gendarme."

"Did she say anything to you at this time?"

"She did tell me not to try to escape," Durand said smiling, "or I would be hunted down like a dog and brought to justice."

"What did you do while she was gone?"

"I just stood there and waited for her to return. I
thought . . . well, never mind . . ."

"What did you think?"

"I thought this woman was bewitched, frankly. And that
it would be a simple matter to explain to the gendarme what
had really happened."

"You made no attempt to leave the premises?"

"Heavens no," Durand declared. "Why should I leave? I
had done nothing."

A general stirring in the direction of the *Société* caused
Judge Remonde to pound his gavel.

"Tell us what happened then."

"In a few minutes, this lady came back dragging a gendarme by the sleeve and demanded that he arrest me."

"Do you remember her exact words?"

"Distinctly. They were entirely too exaggerated. She
said: 'Throw that man in prison.'"

"On what charges?"

"Something about defacing public property."

"What happened then?"

"I tried to explain to the young man what had happened, but she kept waving that pencil in the air and shouting that it was proof positive of my guilt."

"What happened then?"

"Then I was asked, very politely by the young man, to accompany him to the precinct courthouse here. And on this woman's testimony I was assessed a fine of five thousand francs."

"Did you pay this fine?"

"I did not."

"For what reason?"

"Because I was not guilty of the crime. This kind of invasion-of-privacy by citizen groups seemed to me a dangerous precedent to allow. I asked for a trial before a judge, and this was granted."

"One final question. Given the great reverence you have demonstrated for all things artistic, can you imagine yourself, under any circumstances, defacing such a statue in the manner described by the persecution—pardon— the prosecution?"

"Of course not."

"Thank you. Your witness," Montausier said, bowing to Maitre Guinder.

"Monsieur Durand," the prosecutor began. "You state that on the morning in question you went in search of the janitor?"

"Yes, I . . ."

"Is it not true that, as you have stated, you visited the Breville Museum often?"

"Yes, almost . . ."

"Is it not further true that some of these marks existed on the statue in question for quite some time?" Maitre Guinder said, speaking with extreme rapidity.

"Yes, for a . . ."

"Can you in fact ever remember a time when this statue

did not have markings on it?"

"No."

"You had noticed them before, then, is that correct?"

"Oh, heavens yes," Durand chuckled and stopped short at a warning glance from Montausier. He scratched at his temple and shrugged slightly.

"Had you ever thought to complain of this outrage to the janitor before this morning in question?"

"No, but I'm trying . . ."

"But on this morning you decided to report them to the janitor, is that correct?"

"I had thought of . . ."

"But you had not done it, is that correct?"

"I had never been there alone to study . . ."

"Had you or had you not made any previous attempt to report these markings to the janitor?"

"No, but I'm trying . . ."

"But on this morning you decided to report them to the janitor, is that correct?"

"Yes," Durand said emphatically.

"I see," the lawyer paused to allow Durand's apparent inconsistency of behavior to sink in. "I should like to ask if you recall ever laughing over these remarks to some of your friends?"

"I should say not."

"But were you not, only this moment, chuckling over them when I asked you?"

"Objection!" Montausier called out.

"Sustained!" Judge Remonde ruled. "You will please stick to a proper line of questioning, Maitre Guinder," he warned.

"If the court will permit," Maitre Guinder explained. "The prosecution is seeking to establish that Monsieur Durand has never been affronted by these marks, but that he found them, on the contrary, coarsely amusing, as the prosecution intends to show later."

The courtroom bustled with whispers. Judge Remonde's gavel smashed to his desk and he half-heartedly threatened to clear the room.

"Monsieur Durand," Guinder sighed. "Is it not correct that you carry a large stock of contemporary novels in your store?"

"A fairly good stock, yes."

"For the court's information, do you as a bookseller feel a sense of responsibility about the books you sell?" Guinder asked, changing his tone completely as though he asked this out of a genuine interest in learning something about the book business.

"Oh, very much so," Durand said.

"Do you read many of the novels that you have on your shelves?"

"A good sampling, yes."

"You would say, then, that you have some reading knowledge of contemporary fiction?"

"Quite a good knowledge, I should think," Durand said.

"Then I ask you, in view of the incredible filth that one finds in all contemporary novels, and in view of your admitted familiarity with it—how does it happen you could be so affronted by the markings on this statue?" Guinder ground the words out, flushing with anger stirred by his obvious loathing of smut in literature. "They're no different from the junk you sell . . ."

"Objection!" Montausier shouted. "Maitre Guinder is not questioning; he is testifying as a self-styled expert witness in contemporary literature. His contention that all contemporary fiction is filled with 'incredible filth' should not go into the court record unchallenged."

"Sustained," Judge Remonde snapped. "Maitre Guinder, you have a long record as a crusader in this field. I'll ask you to keep your literary prejudices out of my courtroom. Your position is untenable. Take another line of questioning or give up."

"Very well," Guinder said through his heavy breathing.
"Monsieur Durand, is it not correct that you know the janitor
at the Breville Museum personally?"

"I have met him a few times, in the . . ."

"Do you or do you not know him personally?"

"I would not say we were intimate friends or anything
like . . ."

"But you know him rather well?"

"You could say that, I . . ."

"Then did you not know that Wednesday is his day to
leave his post at the Museum a half hour early, at eleven thirty a.m. instead of twelve, in order to take his regular weekly
shot for arthritis at the clinic?"

"I didn't know the poor man was taking shots."

"Remember, you're under oath. Did you not see him, in
fact, from your window across the street, leave early on
Wednesdays, for whatever reason?"

"I may have noticed it."

"Then, were you not—now think carefully—were you
not aware that he was gone from the museum precisely at the
time you claim you went in search of him?"

"I'd forgotten, I suppose."

"I put it to you, Sir, that you went to the Museum knowing that the janitor would be away—that you deliberately
chose that particular time . . ."

"Objection. This is an accusation, not a proper question," Montausier said.

"Sustained. Strike that last from the record," Judge
Remonde ordered.

Maitre Guinder allowed his shoulders to droop, and
looked toward the spectators for sympathy, as though to say
that the court was prejudiced against him.

"Monsieur Durand," he resumed. "You stated for the
newspapers that you grew fatigued and were sitting on the statue to rest your . . ."

"Objection!" Montausier called.

"Sustained. Counsel for the Prosecution knows perfectly well that such unsworn testimony as that provided by newspaper accounts is inadmissible as evidence in this court."

"Monsieur, do you recognize this pencil?" Guinder asked dramatically lifting the brownish object high into the air.

"A pencil is a pencil," Durand said sullenly.

"Is this not your own pencil?"

"I judge it to be the one pilfered from me, but I could not swear it is the same."

"This pencil is marked exhibit B and accepted as evidence."

"Then I suppose it is mine."

"Do you have any doubt that it is yours?"

"I guess not."

"Is it not true that shortly after Madame Hilhaud apprehended you in the act of defacing . . ."

"Objection," Montausier said impatiently. "It has not been proved that the defendant was in the act of defacing anything. I appeal to your honor. This is an unethical tactic to sway the court, and my colleague knows it."

"Sustained!" Judge Remonde cast Maitre Guinder a glance of contempt. "If he doesn't know it, he should go back to law school. You'll find, young man," he said to Guinder, "that your sledge-hammer tactics are not appreciated in this court."

Maitre Guinder raised his hands, palms up, in a hopeless gesture, and then dropped them to his sides loudly.

"Is it not true," he asked in a voice silken with kindness, "that on the morning in question you attempted to wrest this pencil by force from Madame Hilhaud when she took it from you as evidence?"

"She grabbed it from me and I tried to grab it back."

"Would you tell the court why you were so desperate to have this evidence back, desperate enough to attempt to regain it by force and violence?"

"Oh," Durand protested. "I'd hardly say I was violent,

now really."

"Why did you try to get it back unless you were afraid to have it introduced as evidence of your crime?"

"Objection," Montausier said wearily. "It has not been established that my client committed any crime."

"Sustained! I will not tolerate such disreputable courtroom tactics. I don't want to warn you again, Maitre Guinder."

"Why did you try to get this pencil back?" Guinder asked harshly,

"Because it was mine, of course. If someone tried to steal your property, you'd try to get it back, wouldn't you?"

"I'm the one who asks the questions, Sir, if you don't mind. Now, can you honestly say you thought Madame Hilhaud a thief?"

"How was I to know?"

Guinder smiled in Madame Hilhaud's direction, speculatively, as did all of the other members of the *Société* in a manner that attracted the entire courtroom's attention and shouted eloquently that it was entirely too ridiculous to imagine that anyone so spiritual could possibly be a thief."

"This is a common wooden lead-pencil, is it not?" Guinder asked, turning back to Durand and shaking the pencil in the air.

"How much would say it cost?"

"Very little—five or ten francs."

"Less than the price of a postage stamp?"

"I suppose so."

"Ordinarily the loss of one very inexpensive pencil would not be a matter of great concern to you, would it?"

"I guess not," Durand said in a tone of caution.

"Then I wonder if you will tell the Court why you were so terribly concerned to have this particular pencil back."

"Because it was stolen. It was a matter of principle."

"You mean it was seized as evidence, don't you?"

"How was I to know? She just jerked it out of my hand."

"It will be shown later that when Madame Hilhaud seized the pencil, she announced loudly and clearly that it was commandeered as evidence against you. You yourself have already admitted as much," Guinder added blandly.

He carried the pencil to the judge's desk and requested that the judge examine it carefully, particularly the gum end.

"Monsieur Durand, would you not say that the gum end of this pencil still has its square edges?"

"It does."

"Would you not say that if it had been used for marking erasures from marble, the friction would have worn these squared edges to roundness?"

"Yes, but . . ."

"No matter. The point is that this eraser is square—it has not been used."

"The woman pounced on me before I got started," Durand said quickly. He saw Montausier nod approval of his getting that point into the record.

"Thank you. I have no further questions of the witness."

Montausier declined to question further on the points brought out by cross-examination. He called Madame Carnot as his next witness.

When the tobacco-shop proprietress had been sworn in, he asked if she had known Monsieur Durand for some length of time.

"Yes," Madame Carnot answered with dignity. "Many years."

"Would you say that he has been a faithful client?"

"Steady as a rock."

"Would you estimate fidelity to be one of his characteristics?"

"Faithful in one thing, faithful in all, I'd say."

"Did Monsieur Durand come to your shop on the night of Tuesday, January twenty-ninth to make some purchases?"

"He did."

"Did anything occur there, in your presence, that might

give us a further indication of Monsieur Durand's character?"

"It did."

"Will you please tell the court what happened that night."

"Well, a tart came into the store, a woman of obvious ill-fame. She bought a package of cigarettes and made suggestive remarks to Monsieur Durand. He refused to have anything to do with her."

"Did Monsieur Durand say anything to her?"

"Not a word. He just rose above it."

"Would you say he was amused?"

"He was embarrassed and humiliated."

"Was anything said after the woman left?"

"I apologized to him, since the incident occurred in my shop. Like a true gentleman, he absolved me of all blame. He said I was not responsible for the morality of my clients."

"Which is true, of course. Is that all he said?"

"He said for me not to worry—that scum like that'd get their proper reward in hell."

"Were those his exact words?"

"His exact words."

"Did he say anything else about this?" Montausier asked.

Madame Carnot hesitated and glanced toward Durand. His face remained placid under its redness, but his eyes pleaded with her to stop.

"He did," she said apologetically.

"Will you tell the court what else he said."

The tobacconist took a deep breath and spoke with deliberate coldness, as though she hated herself for divulging Durand's intimate confidence. "He told me that never in his life had he had recourse to a prostitute."

Durand's eyes stared into space, in a glaze of agony.

"In your opinion, Madame," Montausier asked loudly above courtroom rustlings, "judging from the speech and actions of the defendant, on the very night before he was apprehended and charged, would you say that he is a man addicted to lewdness?"

"I should say not."

"Would you think that a man who acted with such restraint and propriety in your shop on Tuesday night, would be capable of indulging—the very next night—in the lewdness with which he is here accused?"

"Absolutely not."

"Thank you, Madame. "Your witness," he said, with a nod to Guinder.

"No questions."

While Flamart was being sworn in, the court's attention was distracted by Madame Ponneger who whispered across the table to Maitre Guinder. Judge Remonde tapped his gavel. Maitre Guinder smiled and wrote something on a piece of paper, while Madame Ponneger settled back in her chair with her arms crossed on her breast and smiled with triumphant disdain at the bookseller.

Durand studied her closely. His heart accelerated with recognition. Of course, she was the bat who'd seen him in the movie with the same tart he'd earlier refused at Madam Carnot's. He quickly averted his eyes. Damn. She'd probably been telling Guinder. They would not only nullify the good of Madame Carnot's painful testimony, but would show him up in a way that would disgrace Helene and turn all the women of the quarter against him. He looked back toward Guinder, who scrutinized him with an all-knowing expression of accusation. Durand felt himself wither under the merciless gaze of the Christians.

"Do you know the defendant?" Montausier asked Flamart.

"Yes," Flamart said hoarsely.

"Did you see the defendant at any time last Wednesday, January thirtieth?"

"Yes, in the men's room of the Breville Museum," the stone mason replied.

"You go to the Breville Museum often, it that correct?"

"Every day, almost."

"Please tell the court what happened?"

"I was in there washing. Old Durand over there, he come in. So we got to talking."

"So what did he say?" Flamart smiled uneasily at Montausier, begging for a clue as to what he should say next.

"Take your time," Montausier encouraged. "Did you perhaps discuss the events of the day?"

"Oh, sure—yes, sure that was it. He told me about how he'd opened his shop a little late because he'd taken this bread he bakes over to them monks to eat on."

"Do you mean the bread that Monsieur Durand regularly takes to the young novices at the Dominican house down the street?"

"That's right. He bakes bread for them to eat on."

"I see . . ." Montausier paused to allow for the full impact of this information on the Court.

"He asked me, too, did I see the janitor," Flamart rambled on, searching his memory. "I told him no. That's about all."

"Think carefully. Did he give you any reason why he was looking for the janitor?"

"He did say something about washing that great statue."

"Anything else. "

"Said the marks on her were disgusting."

"Have you known Durand long?"

"Oh God, yes."

"Have you ever know him to participate in any form of lewdness or lasciviousness? Remember, your under oath."

Flamart reddened and fingered his knuckles.

"You mean does he fool around?" he asked finally.

"I mean does he do or say lewd things?"

"You mean fiddle around?"

"Things of that nature, yes."

"Oh God no—you know how he won't even go with us to the . . ."

"That's fine!" Montausier bellowed. "Now, do you feel that you've told us everything that occurred on the morning in question?"

"I think so. He did say one thing, though I don't know if I ought to tell it on him."

"Please tell us what else he said."

Flamart pursed his wrinkled lips and colored to a high blush in his cheeks. "He said something about people making those marks—said they had little respect for great art."

"I see. Thank you. Your witness."

Maitre Guinder rose and strode to the chair in which Flamart sat slumped forward,

"Are you a lover of great art, Monsieur Flamart?"

"Oh God, yes," Flamart said with an affirmative nod.

"Is that why you go to the museum almost every day?"

"Partly."

"You have other reasons?"

"Well, naturally I go to wash up after work," Flamart said, his face unwrinkling in astonishment at such a silly question.

"To wash up after work?"

"But of course. There's soap, water and towels."

"Isn't that dishonest, don't you think?"

"Objection!" Montausier said.

"Sustained. Monsieur Flamart is not on trial here."

"If the court will permit, Counsel for the Prosecution is attempting to establish the honesty of the witness."

"Establish it some other way," Judge Remonde flared.

"What time do you get off from work, Monsieur Flamart?"

"About noon, and again at five."

"If you get off at noon, can you explain what you were doing in the museum washroom at eleven-thirty?"

Flamart turned his head away from the attorney in disgust. "A mason—he don't work in the rain, Monsieur. I thought anybody knew that."

"It rained that morning?"

"But of course it rained that morning."

"You left work early because of the rain?"

"Ask Monsieur Aurey over there. He's my boss. He'll tell you it was really raining."

"Have you ever known Monsieur Durand to laugh at the statue known as *The Reclining Diana?*"

"Oh God, yes."

Montausier tensed forward in his chair.

"You have, is this correct, frequently heard Monsieur Durand laugh at the statue?" Guinder encouraged with a dry chuckle himself.

"But of course," Flamart smiled. "He's a good type when you know him. Very amiable."

"Thank you. No more questions," Maitre Guinder said. He bowed low to Montausier and Durand.

"Do I go now?" Flamart asked.

"Yes," Judge Remonde said gently after receiving an indication that Montausier would not question further. "You may step down."

"You're absolutely certain it's safe to call Madame Ponneger?" Durand asked in panic.

"Yes. You should have told me about this before."

"I didn't know it was her until just this moment."

"Now you've told me everything?—exactly what happened?"

"Yes."

"Good—this should be a coup to lame them properly," Montausier said. He rose and addressed the Judge. "If it please the Court, it has come to our attention only this moment that another person in this courtroom might be capable of shedding some light on the truth. I request that Madame A. Ponneger take the stand."

Activity stirred around Maitre Guinder's table.

"It is our understanding, of course," Montausier taunted, "that Madame Ponneger cannot be obliged to testify in this manner. But we felt that she would be most happy to help clarify the truth and—ah, thank you," Montausier said as Madame Ponneger lumbered to her feet.

"Charity . . ." Father Trissotin reminded in a loud whisper.

Madame Ponneger ignored Maitre Guinder's warming frown. She marched to the chair and defiantly lifted her right hand to be sworn.

"Thank you, Madame, for your kind cooperation," Montausier saluted her when she took her seat. "Do you know the defendant, Monsieur Durand, personally?"

"I should say not!"

"Have you ever seen him before?"

"Oh yes," she said ominously, and reached up to pick at the shoulders of her dress with great energy.

"Is it true that on last Tuesday night, January 29, you attended the Cine Olympia?"

"I did. As part of my duties for the *Société*, I saw Monsieur Smut-Peddler himself there," she said in a loud voice, smiling toward her group.

"If you're referring to the defendant, Monsieur Durand, we object to your continued use of the words 'smut peddler.'"

"Object all you want."

Judge Remonde warned her to watch her language or risk a contempt of court charge.

"Might I ask if there was anything unusual about Monsieur Durand's attending the movie? The movie, as I understand it, was the Charlie Chaplin Revival. A perfectly innocent way for a man to spend the evening, is it not?"

"Not when he was in the company of a tart young enough to be his daughter."

Durand stared intently at his hands and heard the courtroom tense to silence around him.

"Madame Ponneger," Montausier gasped, feigning confusion.

"It was obviously that girl he had so gallantly refused at

Madame Carnot's only a few moments before . . . one of
Madame Culuhac's . . ."

Judge Remonde pounded his gavel furiously. "Strike that
last phrase from the record," he shouted to the impassive
court reporter. "Madame Culuhac is not on trial here. Your
implication that she illegally harbors tarts will not be admitted. Neither will your unproven suspicions that the defendant's companion was the same woman whose solicitation
Durand had previously refused."

"Well, for heavens sake—everybody knows Madame
Culuhac runs a house of . . ."

"Strike!" Judge Remonde ordered. "I will not tolerate
this sort of character defamation in my court. Madame
Culuhac is not accused of . . ."

"She will be soon enough," Madame Ponneger interrupted. She flopped around in her chair to face her group, with
her back half-turned to the judge. She grabbed her shoulder
seam and gave it a vicious yank.

"In any case," Montausier resumed mournfully. "You
contend Monsieur Durand was in the company of a girl who
was, in your opinion, a person of easy virtue."

"She was a tart—no question about that. She even
admitted it right there in the theater."

"Oh come now, Madame . . . "

"She did, I'm telling you."

"How did she admit it?"

"I don't use that kind of language," Madame Ponneger
announced.

"The Court orders you to answer Maitre Montausier's
question," Judge Remonde said. "How did she admit she was
a tart?"

"She said she'd slept with the nobility, if you must
know," Madame Ponneger lashed out.

"Perhaps she was married to a Count or a Baron,"
Montausier suggested.

"Don't be funny. She admitted it, I'm telling you."

"She did not, however, admit who might be harboring her?" Judge Remonde put in.

"No, but it's obvious, isn't it?"

"Madame. . ." he warned.

"You asked for the truth for heaven's sakes!"

"We're having a hard time getting it," Remonde muttered.

"Very well," Montausier continued. "We have it established that the defendant was seated in the Cine Olympia in the company of an admitted prostitute—is that correct?"

"Of course it's correct. That's what I've been saying. It was the most lecherous display of lewdness I ever saw."

"What exactly did you see? Was Monsieur Durand touching this girl in any way?"

"In the dark how could I tell?"

"Well, then, how do you know anything was happening at all?"

"They turned on the lights," Madame Ponneger answered.

"When they turned on the lights was Monsieur Durand touching her in any way?"

"No, but he was certainly talking to her."

"Did you hear what he said?"

"Of course I did—most disgusting thing I've ever heard."

Judge Remonde struck his gavel. He bent over his desk and glared at her. "Will you please answer the question and stop giving your reactions. What might well disgust you and me possibly will not disgust the laws of justice." The old man nodded curtly to Montausier to continue.

"May I ask if this girl solicited Monsieur Durand?"

"Apparently she did."

"And did he accept her solicitation?"

"No!"

"A grave personal disappointment to you, no doubt?"

"Why you . . ."

"Objection," shouted Maitre Guinder.

"Sustained," Judge Remonde sighed. "Strike counsel's last statement. Counsel will please confine himself to a proper line of questioning."

"Is it not true, Madame?" Montausier asked with dramatic slowness, "that Monsieur Durand's exact words in reply to the woman's advances were: 'Get out of here and leave me alone?'"

"Oh I don't remember the exact words."

"Would you at least say that his behavior and language were of such a nature as to leave no doubt in the onlooker's mind that, in effect, Monsieur Durand not only refused this woman's immoral advances, but that he literally drove her from the theater for even suggesting such a thing?"

"Yes, but it didn't give that impression at all."

"In effect, however, is it not substantially correct that he refused her, and further that he told her to get out and leave decent people alone—to go peddle her wares elsewhere?"

"Yes, but it didn't *sound* that way," Madame Ponneger said in desperation. "Can't you understand—he was just showing off!"

"Is not a virtuous man supposed to display his virtue as an example to humanity? Even were he showing-off, which is merely your personal opinion, Madame, was this not the time and place to show-off, to show the world that he was not afraid to drive the money-changers from the temple?"

"Oh Lord," Madame Ponneger moaned.

"As the facts show us, would you not say that a person with lewd characteristics would not get very far with Monsieur Durand?"

"Lord no, I wouldn't say that. I tell you he was enjoying the whole thing. He even grinned once."

"Have you ever heard the admonition that we should rejoice in our virtue?"

"Yes, but . . ."

"Thank you, Madame. That is all."

Spontaneous applause clattered through the courtroom

as Montausier turned and strode grandly to his chair. Judge Remonde smashed his gavel against the pounding board and threatened to clear the court if there were any further outbursts from the spectators.

Maitre Guinder refused the privilege of questioning Madame Ponneger further.

Durand watched her heavy hips roll slowly as she walked back to her group. His jubilation over Montausier's masterful interrogation was tempered with vague pity, for the faces of her group left no doubt that she was being charitably dismembered in their minds and that later she would be dismembered in their conversations.

Even Father Trissotin's face bore the exaggerated expression of betrayed dignity, distant and withdrawn, as though he hoped to give the impression that he did not know who these women were.

28

"Any more questions?" Father Gregoire asked. He looked over the narrow room where young men sat behind long desk-like tables taking notes from his regular afternoon conference.

"Very well," he said when no one spoke. "Now, we're going to change our schedule today, because this is the feast of St. Martha and it's turning into a cold and nasty day. Also, since the doctor has ordered Lupe to take some mid-afternoon nourishment and God has seen fit to move Monsieur Durand to bring us magnificent bread, you're all invited to the kitchen for a nice meal. Friar Lupe will have poached eggs, wheat bread and tea. The rest of us will have warmed tartines of Monsieur Durand's bread, with some honey and butter, and bowls of that obscenity that Father Cuisinier calls coffee. All right, let's go." Robes rustled down the somber corridor as

rapidly as walking permitted without becoming running.
Father Gregoire felt the currents of lightness and enthusiasm
flow out from the wordless group.

Though they had not been told of Lupe's condition,
Father wondered again that such knowledges appear to
emanate from the walls in a monastery, for certainly all of
them surmised the truth.

As they entered the kitchen door, the odor of Durand's
warming bread intensified their preoccupation with Lupe's
death, and added to the festive lightness, as though it cleansed
their hearts of all doubts and purified the love that brought
them there. Father Gregoire switched on the lights to provide
as much cheer as possible. The dryness and fragrance of the
room, warmed by the ovens, encouraged talk, and the Prior
made no attempt to dampen it.

Muffled through many walls, the four o'clock bells from
the clock tower filtered indistinctly to them.

29

Madame Hilhand pressed her fingertips against her ears
to shut out the great bell's room-shattering clangor. She
stepped from the witness stand after her brief but vehement
testimony.

Maitre Guinder, flushed with the damning implications
he had elicited from her, shouted loudly above the noise for his
next witness, Monsieur Aurey.

Durand glanced toward Flamart whose eyes blinked in
surprise to note that his boss was taking the stand against his
best friend.

"Have you ever seen the defendant before?" Guinder
asked.

"Oh yes—frequently over at the Cafe Zeus," Monsieur
Aurey beamed with much the same felicity Durand remem-

bered from the younger Aurey's visit that morning. "He's there almost every evening with his friends. Then, too, I've occasionally bought books from him at his shop."

"Does he habitually meet the same people at the Cafe?"

"Oh yes—always the same two. Montausier, his lawyer there, and old Flamart the stone mason who works for me."

"Is there anything significant about these meetings you would like to mention here?"

"I have nothing at all against Durand as a person. I believe in the basic goodness of my fellow man." Aurey smiled and glanced toward the ladies of the *Société*. "But let's not paint him quite so much the saint, eh? We're all more or less human, after all."

"Objection," Montausier called. "Surely Monsieur Aurey was not called to the stand to give us the benefit of these homely observations."

"Sustained. The Court wishes facts."

"Well," Aurey said with a glare at Montausier for his humiliating remark. "If you want facts, I can tell you that only last week at the Cafe Zeus I heard Monsieur Durand in a violent argument about morals with Maitre Montausier. Durand made an eloquent and cynical plea for greater latitude in our moral codes. Montausier, who defends him here today, was in bitter opposition to the bookseller's viewpoint on morality only a week ago!"

Durand cast a pained look at Montausier before a disturbance in the courtroom attracted his attention. A short, heavily-built young man hurried up the aisle and embraced Durand on both cheeks. Durand indicated an empty chair at the defense table for his son.

"Can you recall precisely what was said?" Maitre Guinder asked.

"Not precisely, but—well, it was enough to make me realize that they've stretched Monsieur Durand's virtue beyond all reality here today."

"In sum," Maitre Guinder soothed, "the conversation

you over-heard at the Cafe Zeus would lead you to suspect that at best Monsieur Durand is something less than virtuous in his moral views?"

"Objection!" Montausier called.

"Sustained. Let's have a more specific line of questioning."

"Now just take your time, Monsieur Aurey," Guinder said. "Can you tell us something more specific about the argument?"

"Well, Montausier was berating people for being so immoral these days. He said he had great contempt for all humanity—some because they were villains and others, like Durand, because he was complacent toward them and even showed a certain respect for sin."

Montausier's sigh of defeat spread over the courtroom. He gazed with exaggerated sadness at his hands in his lap. Durand reached over and placed his hand on Julien's powerful shoulder to quell the boy's fury.

"Did Monsieur Durand give any answer to this rather significant condemnation made against him by the very man who is here today attempting to prove to us the limpidity of his character and morals?" Maitre Guinder asked triumphantly.

"He did—yes. He said something about the great stiffness of the morality of past ages being against the grain of modern times. He said Montausier looked rather ridiculous raging against immorality. And if I recollect correctly, he said that we must not demand too much perfection from mortals, but must take them as they are."

Madame Ponneger whispered into Father Trissotin's ear. The priest smiled broadly and nodded his head, no longer ashamed to be identified with the *Société*. Montausier could not repress a glance of amusement in Durand's direction while from the corner of his eye he watched Judge Remonde stare pensively toward the ceiling, as though Aurey's words were somehow familiar to him.

"Can you recall anything else that was specifically stated

by the defendant?"

"No, it was all in that line. Montausier was on the side of strict morality and Durand was against him and made fun of morality. After that they got to talking about baking bread."

"Judging from what you have told us," Guinder asked. "Would you think that Monsieur Durand would find the markings on the statue in the Breville Museum gravely offensive?"

"No."

"Thank you. Your witness, Maitre," Guinder said with a curt nod toward Montausier.

"Monsieur Aurey," Montausier began with a hopeless shrug. "Will you state your age."

"Fifty-four."

"Will you tell the Court something about your schooling?"

"I attended the Lycée St. Maurice and then the College of Industrial Engineering."

"You studied literature in the lycée, did you not?"

"Oh, yes, of course."

"Was it not the practice in such classes to have students act out different parts of the plays you studied?"

"That's right."

"A fine system, isn't it? I ask you this because you and the defendant Durand are about the same age, and I know it was the custom in his lycée as it was in mine. You were obliged to memorize your role and act it out?"

"Yes. . ."

"Do you remember some of the roles you acted?"

"Goodness yes. I played Doña Josefa in *Hernani* and Hippolite in *Phaedre* and . . ."

"Those are important roles. You must have been good."

"I suppose I did have a certain—Oh, I wouldn't say I was good. You don't see me on the roster of the *Comedie Française*," Aurey laughed, disarmed by the relaxed manner of Montausier's interrogation.

"Tell me, do you find you still remember some of those

parts learned in your school days?"

"Yes, it's unbelievable really. I suppose that things memorized in youth remain with us the longest. Sometimes I find myself quoting entire passages."

"A very enriching background," Montausier said in quiet admiration. "Now, if we can return to the testimony just presented. Would you say that the argument between Monsieur Durand and me was pleasant—a friendly debate?"

"I thought it was explosive."

"You think that feelings were aroused?"

"No question about it. You were terribly flushed there at one point if you remember."

"Judging then, from what you overheard at the Cafe Zeus, would you—and I ask you to think very carefully—say that a man who would utter such statements was of a more or less unmoral disposition?" Montausier asked sadly.

"I would say that such statements reflect badly—yes, very badly—on the character of the man making them. They scandalized me, frankly, and I'm no prude."

"Would you then say that he has a shameful character?"

"I'm afraid so."

"You would condemn him for such utterances?"

"Most certainly. I mean there are limits. It is unforgivable to tear down morality or even—I suppose—to make light of it."

Montausier stepped directly in front of Judge Remonde's desk. "If it please the Court," he said calmly. "We have just heard a most eloquent testimony in condemnation not of my client, Charles Durand, but—as every schoolboy knows—of one of the recognized glories of France—the great Molière!"

"I knew those lines were familiar," Judge Remonde blurted out.

"The inexact quotes now on record and attributed to Monsieur Durand might well be, for the sake of literature, corrected as follows:

> *The great stiffness of the morality of past ages*
> *Is against the grain of our century and our usages.*

Then Montausier's voice rang out:

> *It demands of mortals too much perfection.*
> *We must bend with the times, without obstination.*

Madame Ponneger's face congested slowly as she realized how Montausier had tricked Monsieur Aurey into condemning no less a person than Molière.

"They have been had!" someone shouted from the back of the courtroom, above laughter and applause, above an outraged shushing.

Judge Remonde expressed his admiration in a glance at Montausier and pounded for order.

"The scene described by Monsieur Aurey," Montausier continued, addressing the Judge, "was more or less filled with lines we learned in literature classes long ago when we were schoolboys. We meet frequently at the cafe to engage in friendly debate on all subjects—as a stimulus to our minds. The evening in question, our debate happened to fall on the subject that Molière satirizes in his masterpiece, *Le Misanthrope*. Our language automatically became his language—the speeches from Act One which we were apparently studying at school at about the same time Monsieur Aurey was starring in schoolboy productions."

Montausier resumed a severe attitude and spoke harshly. "Once again I request a dismissal of this case on the grounds that all of the statements of the prosecution have been reduced to absurdities, as proved by the fact that we have ended up in the ridiculous position of having to listen to testimony not against my client, but against Molière."

"Request denied. Are there further witnesses?"

"None." Maitre Guinder mumbled.

"Do you wish to sum up?"

Durand watched Monsieur Aurey shrug his shoulders in answer to Madame Ponneger's accusing glare, as if to say: "How was I know?" He saw Madame Aurey reach over and take her husband's hand.

"If it please the court," Maitre Guinder began in a lusterless voice. "We have proved that Monsieur Durand was at the scene of the crime at the time indicated. Witnesses have testified to this and Monsieur Durand has admitted it. Now, defense counsel Montausier has sought to turn this court of law into a circus by his clever entrapment of my witnesses, but it must be obvious that such antics prove his complete lack of sincerity. Indeed, such antics fool no one—certainly they do not conform to the picture of the defendant Durand as a man of unimpeachable morality and stratospheric ideals. I suggest that they prove the opposite—there has been an undertone of the ludicrous that can only make Monsieur Durand's vaunted morality show up in its true light of cynicism. Montausier has even been naïve enough to attempt to persuade this court that a man of Monsieur Durand's obvious worldliness was so affronted by obscene markings on a statue—markings he had seen countless times before, remember—that he was suddenly overwhelmed by an emotion never previously obsessive with him; an emotion of civic pride, if you please, that he set about to erase those marks. The fact and the whole tenor of this hearing can leave no doubt in our minds as to the real truth. Monsieur Durand was apprehended in the act. He was caught with a pencil in his hand. His claim that he intended to erase the marks simply does not hold up in view of his past proved amusement at them."

Maitre Guinder faced the judge's desk and spoke loudly. "Therefore, for the good of this community, for the good of this entire land, I ask you to return a verdict of guilty. If ridicule is heaped on the sincere testimony and sincere efforts of this *Société*, it will only give the petty vandals and pornographers and immoralists more complacency and encourage an atmosphere of lasciviousness corrupting to all young people. A cold view of the public morality in this age of sensuality must terrify all decent souls. To correct it, anyone apprehended in acts of an obscene nature—regardless of the wit and trickery of his defending counsel—must be relentlessly punished. All France awaits your decision, your Honor. The decent parents of little children watch and pray that you will act here today to stop this kind of filth and to justify groups like our *Société*. The morally degraded watch, too, breath-bated to see if you, by deciding in favor of Durand, will in effect tell them that they are free to deprave public morals to their heart's content. I thank you."

"Does counsel for the Defense wish to sum up?"

Montausier rose and immediately began speaking, even as he walked toward the judge's desk. "Justice is based on facts and on truth derived from those facts," he said with lofty confidence. "The prosecution here seeks the punishment of a scapegoat on the premise that if he is punished—whether guilty or not—it will serve notice on others not to contemplate crimes similar to those of which he is unjustly accused—but which he never contemplated himself. Look at the inconsistency. Here, ironically, a religious group is willing to go against a first principle of morality which teaches us that we can never be justified in using an evil means to gain a good end. Did they ask for justice? No, they asked that my client be relentlessly punished. Why? To serve the good end, yes, the admirable end, of deterring petty vandals and pornographers and immoralists, but how? By the evil means of seeking an unjust decision against my client, Durand."

"As for the markings on the statue, we wish to call these facts to your attention. First, the statue is covered with such markings. Second, it has been established that my client could not have been seated on the statue's pedestal for more than thirty seconds. No one has been able to specify a single marking as the one allegedly put there by my client; and obviously he could not possibly have made *all* of them in that short time. So they have presented not one shred of true evidence to prove

that Monsieur Durand actually made, or even thought of making, any lewd, lascivious, obscene or immoral markings on this
masterpiece.

"In summation, then, we have a generalized picture of a
man who has never been known to participate in any form of
lewd activity, but who on at least two occasions showed his
contempt for persons who proposed such activities to him. We
have the picture of a man who has always quietly espoused
noble causes—the sort of man who bakes bread for the
Dominicans and the sort of man who refused to be intimidated
by economic pressures and threats of boycott into submitting
to the *Société*'s program to castrate literature. This takes rare
courage and illustrates devotion to an ideal. We see his further
respect for art and his community spirit in such characteristic
gestures as the Maritain poster. Is it even remotely logical to
think a man who has done all of these things to elevate art in
his community would be likely to deface a great piece of marble statuary?"

"To conclude, we wish to make it clear that we do not
insult the Court by asking for a verdict based on some ulteri-
or motive of face-saving or setting a 'good example' for the
community. Justice is the best possible example we can set
here."

A growing scatter of applause caused Judge Remonde to
tap his gavel lightly.

"If there has been an element of the ridiculous here, as
the opposition contends," Montausier went on loudly, "then
the actions of the prosecuting group have made it so. The
prude and the bigot are always ridiculous because they are
willing to commit crimes against human liberty on the pretext
their acts are dictated by moral virtue. But moral virtue is
impossible without the intellectual virtues of prudence and
understanding which direct man to the *proper* means of
achieving his goals. They would rob Peter to pay Paul. And
they would rob Durand, for it is as great a crime against justice to rob a man of his good name as it is to steal his goods. In

the same way they would rob the community of access to great literature—and God knows what else—in order to protect our virtue. In other words they would impoverish us spiritually in order to protect us spiritually."

"No, we do not ask for face-saving decisions. We ask for a verdict that most perfectly conforms to Justice, certain that such a verdict will best preserve our individual freedoms from the well-meaning but nonetheless dictatorial oppression of such groups. We ask for justice. Nothing more. Nothing less. I thank you."

Montausier bowed first to the judge and then to the applauding audience. He resumed his seat and glanced at the notebook to see if he had forgotten any salient points.

30

Madame Culuhac looked down through large snowflakes on the heads and shoulders of the of the jubilant crowd that emerged from the courtroom next door. She opened her window to listen.

Yes, no doubt about it. Durand had won. Madame relaxed against the window jamb a moment, inhaling the icy air, and basked in the relief this news brought her.

Slowly the mood of relief modulated to one of festivity. She closed her window and turned on her neon sign to enliven the street's twilight gloom. She crossed the room and stood above her hot-plate. Yes, she would aromatize the prunes with the subtlest hint of kirsch, serve them with a tartine of bread and sweet butter, and have a glass of that good heavy Pommard. And yes, she would do it right. She would set the table for her own private little celebration of Durand's victory over "the powers of darkness" as Montausier had called them. A linen cloth, her best silver, candles—she would eat in style.

31

"Then it is agreed that we disband?" Mademoiselle Mailleferre asked, attempting to feign disappointment over a heart impatient for the almost unbearable excitement of going upstairs to the fire she had told Claudine to set in the hearth.

"There's nothing else we can do," Father Trissotin said in a similar tone of disappointment. But his voice betrayed the hint of eagerness to get home to his Aunt Louise's cooking, to enjoy supper and then a protracted quiet time. He leaned against a counter of statues of St. Jude Thaddeus and averted his face from Madame Ponneger's sharp scrutiny. "Obviously, if Durand is serious about his suit for damages against the *Société*, we must either disband or face the fact that we will have to pay the damages, and . . ."

"Where would we ever get one million francs?" Mademoiselle Toulenc asked.

"Can't we fight this thing?" Madame Ponneger bellowed. "If we won, we wouldn't have to pay."

"No chance, I'm afraid," Father Trissotin said. "Maitre Guinder, for all his wonderful qualities, is no match for Montausier."

"In my opinion," Madame Aurey said carefully, "we will have to scrape to get the money to pay the court costs for this trial. I know Monsieur Aurey is going to be most . . ."

"Imagine that Judge Remonde assessing us all cost," Madame Hilhaud said bitterly.

"And talking like he did—scolding us like we were children."

"No—there is only one way out," Father Trissotin said. "We must at least temporarily disband."

"All in favor of disbanding say 'Aye,' Mademoiselle

Mailleferre said, pulling her coat closer around her against the cold of her shop. "The 'ayes' have it. The *Société* is now formally dissolved and the minutes, treasurer's report and other remnants will be turned over to the diocese to become part of its historical file."

"Well, I'm wondering," Madame Aurey said with maddening slowness, "what I should do with all those pamphlets my husband and son have been distributing to the men's rooms."

"Do you have many?" Father Trissotin asked.

"Heavens yes. And more on order."

"Well, I'd like to have my own pamphlets back. I like to keep a good stock on hand."

"All right. But what about the other ones?"

"Any of you ladies want them?" Father asked. "No? Well, you might give them to some charitable institution."

"I think this is disgusting!" Madame Ponneger exploded. "Are we to go down in defeat like this? What about our plans to bash that Goudimel? I thought you were so thrilled with the action we were taking . . ."

Father Trissotin smiled lamely. "Let's look at it this way. All of us have done a heartfelt job. Perhaps there have been some errors. Perhaps God moves in stranger ways than we imagine. Who knows? We cannot continue unless we are prepared to go through another trial, which I do not think we could possibly win. It is not a matter of spirit, but of finances. We must accept God's manifest will in this."

"Father's right. It's really the only thing to do," Mademoiselle Mailleferre affirmed. "Now I suppose that since we're all freezing to death down here, we end this emergency meeting and all go home and have a good supper and forget."

"Well, you certainly are taking this philosophically," Madame Ponneger accused. "You act almost glad."

"No, of course not. Now, I declare this final meeting adjourned," Mademoiselle Mailleferre said, stirred to a vague and amused pity by impatience despite her pleasant reassurances that it had been inspiring to work with such a group.

When they had gone, she bolted the door and switched off the light in her shop. In a profound settling of nerves, she leaned against the window jamb, savoring the silence, the darkness. Past St. Joseph's shoulder, as her eyes accustomed to the obscurity, she saw the feeble glow of the street lamp in front of the Dominicans. She watched the downshifting of golden snowflakes across the lamp's halo as though the sight were a miracle, seeing it all fresh, all new.

After a long moment she turned and made her way in darkness through aisles of religious objects, moved to felicity by the idea of going to her room to sit before a fire in the hearth.

32

"Turn it up a little, will you?" Durand called as he stirred brown sugar into the warm yeasty milk.

"All right," Julien said. Music of Offenbach filled the apartment, drowning the roar of Helene's bathwater.

Durand dipped his forefinger into the liquid and tasted the mingled flavors of flesh and tobacco and bread leaven. Yes, it could not fail. The premonition was there before any of the brown flour had been added. It was the reaction of a master, he told himself. Well, here he was a great patron of the arts, a man of unsullied morality. Well, it made a man feel good.

He bent over the sink to open the sack of wheat flour when the telephone rang. A moment later, Julien reported that Mama would not be over tonight—too nasty out.

Good. Now Durand could stay home and bake the week's bread supply for himself and the Dominicans. He thought of Lupe in his cell and of his Julien. Such different types and yet they intermingled in his affections. Both of them, along with

Helene, were somehow involved in his baking. They made fruitful all his skill, his knowledge and art, merely by taking his bread into their bodies and allowing it to nourish their tissues.

Durand listened to the music and smelled the fragrance of yeast and wheat and molasses that escaped in bubbles from the dough's surface as he kneaded. He felt the stove warm his backside as he worked, content with the dream of evening, content to be there with his family, safely inside while the night lived its own life out there in snowfall and darkness.

33

Father Gregoire woke to the immense silence. An odor of clean straw surrounded him from his mattress. He listened for Lupe's cough, but the corridor remained silent.

Were others in other cells awake too and listening? Each was alone in himself this night, alone in his deepest solitude, in attitudes of sleep or wakefulness or prayer or simple awareness of the presence of God in their souls.

Father Gregoire dragged himself from the warmth of his cover. He would go sit by Lupe's bed for a time. Others who might be awake would hear his footsteps. It would bring them peace to know he was there should Lupe need water or medicine. He carried a blanket to put around his shoulders.

34

The luminosity of an unbroken cloud mass, lighted by the full moon beyond, suffused Madame Ponneger's bedroom. She lay in the deep comfort of her bed. Her gaze wandered over the rounded featherbed comforter to the hearth where coals glowed pink in the grate; and then to the colder sight of enormous snowflakes that floated past her window. She glanced at the crucifix that hung on the flowered wall beside her bed, monochrome in the moon-fogged room.

The great bell from the clock tower clanged out midnight. Madame listened and wondered who else in the quarter might be awake at this hour, hearing these beautiful cathedral-like masses of golden sound. Perhaps Father Trissotin? Perhaps the ladies . . . But no, no use thinking about them. She focused her attention on the distant metallic reverberations that quavered away to the silence of snow falling over the roof tops of the quarter.

Madame Ponneger finally closed her eyes and, reflecting on ridding the quarter of smut, listened to her own large voice sigh in the unearthly hush of her room: "Shit."

finis

About the Author:
John Howard Griffin

Known primarily as the author of the modern classic, *Black Like Me*, John Howard Griffin was also a critically-acclaimed novelist and essayist, a remarkable photographer and musicologist, and a dynamic lecturer and teacher.

Internationally respected as an effective human rights activist, Griffin worked with the Reverend Dr. Martin Luther King and Dick Gregory in the South and with Saul Alinsky and NAACP Director Roy Wilkins in the North during the Civil Rights era. He taught seminars at the University of Peace with Nobel Peace Laureate Father Dominique Pire in Belgium, and delivered hundreds of lectures worldwide. After *Black Like Me*, he wrote more radical works on black liberation and white racism, including *The Church and the Black Man* and *A Time To Be Human*. He was the recipient of many humanitarian honors, as well as awards in the arts.

During a decade of blindness, from Easter 1947 until January 1957, he wrote novels and short stories. His first novel, *The Devil Rides Outside* (1952), was a bestseller and a test case in a controversial censorship trial that was settled in his favor by the US Supreme Court. *Nuni*, a second novel, was published in 1956 and *Land of the High Sky*, a history of West Texas, appeared in 1959. Later works, including books about Thomas Merton (*Follow the Ecstasy* and *The Hermitage Journals*) and *Encounters With the Other*, were published posthumously.

Griffin was recognized for his magnificent black & white portraits of fabled artists like tenor Roland Hayes, pianists Arthur Rubinstein and Lili Kraus, cellist Zara Nelsova, poets Pierre Reverdy, Mark Van Doren and Denise Levertov, folksinger Josh White, and painter Andrew Dasburg. He also created photographic books: *A Hidden Wholeness: The Visual World of Thomas Merton*; and *Jacques Maritain: Homage in Words and Pictures*.

As a classically-trained musician, he studied composition with Nadia Boulanger and Robert Cassadesus and researched religious music at the Abbey of Solesmes—all in France. As a musicologist, he lectured and published on many musical topics, and he was recognized as an authority on the Gregorian Chant.

Author of the Introduction:
Robert Bonazzi

Robert Bonazzi wrote the definitive work to date on John Howard Griffin, the critically-acclaimed *Man in the Mirror: John Howard Griffin and the Story of Black Like Me* (Orbis Books, NY 1997), hailed by Jonathan Kozol as "a beautiful and stirring portrait." As representative for the Griffin Estate, he authored a new afterword for Penguin's 35th anniversary edition of *Black Like Me*, edited and introduced Griffin's *Encounters with the Other* and *Follow the Ecstasy: The Hermitage Years of Thomas Merton*, and has written about Griffin for American Legacy, The New York Times, Bloomsbury Review, Motive, National Catholic Reporter, Merton Seasonal, Texas Observer, as well as periodicals in Germany, France, England, Canada and Mexico.

His poetry, fiction and criticism have appeared in 200 international publications. "Light Casualties"—a short story about Vietnam published by Transatlantic Review of London—was cited in *Vietnam War Literature* and *The Best American Short Stories of 1969*. *The Musical Erotic*, a novella, was published in New York and Mexico City in 1975. Other fiction has appeared in The Village Voice, TriQuarterly, Minnesota Review, Chelsea, Granite, New Letters, New Orleans Review and several anthologies.

His books of poetry include *Living the Borrowed Life* (New Rivers Press, NY, 1974), *Fictive Music: Prose Poems 1975-1977* (Wings Press, 1979), *Domingo* and *Perpetual Texts* (Latitudes, 1974 and 1985). A volume of new and selected poems, *The Scribbling Cure*, is scheduled for publication in 2002. Bonazzi currently lives in San Francisco and is working on *Humane Rites*, portraits of activists, and *Wisdom Gathers Slowly*, a memoir about mentors.

About the Cover Artist:
Abraham Rattner

New York expressionist painter Abraham Rattner—who lived for twenty years in Paris and knew Picasso, Braque, Miró, Giacometti, Rouault, Soutine, Gris, Le Corbusier and Dali—was a devout Jew and an artist of the spirit. "I would recommend to those who desire to be initiated into the Temple," he wrote, "to consider that art belongs to the spirit, and partakes of the nature of religion." Biblical figures and themes, like the cover painting of Moses used on *Street of the Seven Angels*, were a central focus throughout his career.

In a letter to his friend and fellow exile, novelist Henry Miller, Rattner wrote: "I say it is by the grace of God, that's all. Yes, I pray each night before I close my eyes; I pray each morning . . . and talk to God and ask for his guidance, direction, clarity, that I may be able to perceive and feel something that which becomes beauty."

The heart of his credo—that "the work becomes a created one as the artist forgets self, and the good work of art must not be subordinated to the personal good of the artist"—influenced Griffin's view of art. He had met Rattner and French musicians Robert Cassadesus, Nadia Boulanger and Francis Poulenc at the mansion of a schoolmate, cubist painter Jacques Duthoos, whose wealthy family were patrons of the arts in Tours.

After Griffin had escaped a Nazi death squad in 1939, he served three years in the US Air Force in the Pacific theatre, and continued to correspond with Rattner, Cassadesus and Father Marie-Bruno. After the war he returned to France by way of New York to pick up a package from Rattner for the French poet Pierre Reverdy, which Griffin delivered while making a retreat at the Abbey of Solesmes to study Gregorian Chant in 1947.

Colophon

The first edition of *Street of the Seven Angels*, by John Howard Griffin, is printed on 70 pound non-acidic Arbor paper, containing fifty percent post-consumer recycled fiber, by Edwards Brothers, Inc. of Ann Arbor, Michigan. Text and interior titles were set in a contemporary version of Classic Bodoni, originally designed by the 18th century Italian typographer and punchcutter, Giambattista Bodoni, press director for the Duke of Parma. *Street of the Seven Angels* was entirely designed by Bryce Milligan.

Wings Press was founded in 1975 by J. Whitebird and Joseph F. Lomax as "an informal association of artists and cultural mythologists dedicated to the preservation of the literature of the nation of Texas." The publisher/editor since 1995, Bryce Milligan is honored to carry on and expand that mission to include the finest in American writing.